# REALM OF SHADOWS

## CLINT WESTGARD

# ALSO BY CLINT WESTGARD

Published by Lost Quarter Books
www.lostquarterbooks.com

Cover image : Deranged Doctor Designs
ISBN: 1928035035
ISBN-13: 978-1-928035-03-9

*For my family, for all their support.*

# CONTENTS

# PRINCIPAL CHARACTERS

## *Craitol:*

### Lastl:

*Donier a Fieled, noble of the third rank, officer in the Gver's army*

*Keleprai a Lastl, Gver of Lastl*

*Kigarle a Nepene, noble of the first rank in Lastl*

*Liene ul Terainous a Fusel, noble of rank in Lastl*

*Ludenn a Ghuerl, noble of rank, officer in the Gver's army*

*Niriese ul Keleprai a Vellar, wife of the Gver of Lastl*

### Craitol:

*Alieren, Qraulla of the Realm*

*Dalenna ul Lestulatera, mother to the Qraul*

*Elihaun, Master of Offices for the Qraul*

*Laterala, Qraul of the Realm*

### Other Great Families:

*Byuvir a Kylep, Gver of Kylep*

*Duirhe a Takyl, Gver of Takyl*

*Pervelte a Pysel, Gver of Pysel*

Adepts:

*Cepedutherupt, High Adept of the Council of Adepts*

*Hieran, disciple to Adept Tehh*

*Kercubegahedd, false Adept and leader of the Kragian rebellion*

*Tehh, Adept of Lastl*

*Vyissan, a Kragian and an Adept*

## *Renuih:*

*Ad Eselte, emperor of Renuih*

Ad Ezern:

*Ctuellan, eunuch*

*Ibrazol id Ezern, Imperial Vazeir*

*Masiph den Ibrazol id Ezern, Jetthir of the Watch, son of Ibrazol*

Ad Reteln:

*Nyzrella (Nyzren) id Reteln, daughter of Osiphan*

*Osiphan id Reteln, nohritai in Darrhyn*

*Quesin, eunuch*

*Tequihan, castulan of the Ad Reteln household*

*Usyre id Reteln ys Luzyren, wife of Osiphan*

Nohritai:

*Erise id Illied, wife of Nustef*

*Gheyuth id Lelletl, Vazeir of the Renian Army*

*Nustef id Illied, second to Masiph on the Watch, husband of Erise*

*Achelluth, member of the Watch*

*Fush, sutler in the Renian army*

*Nazeed, one of Osiphan's conspirators*

*Phariayh, camp follower in the Renian army*

# ONE:

# THE QUIET OF THE NIGHT

# 1

Clouds blanketed the sky, rippling bruises in the twilight. The city Darrhyn below, sprawling along the bend of a wide river, was draped in the resultant shadows, pierced only intermittently by the remnants of the day's sun. Hurried figures passed from street to street in certain of its quarters to light the lamps, while others were left to what the night would bring. Along the city's great wall the beacons in the towers were struck, signaling the changing of the Watch. The new quadras marched up tower stairs, the soldiers heading out to pace the ramparts, looking into the final glare of the sun as it cast the scrub of the desert in oranges and reds.

Within one of the watchtowers five men squinted in the lamplight at a just-overturned cup, none of them speaking. Above them the sentinel on duty was singing an academy song about a woman so light in her manners that she would invite any man to sup with her.

"Call," the dealer said as he removed his hand from the cup, its contents still a mystery.

The youth to his left exhaled slowly as he eyed the cup. "Even. Five kenir," he said, the flames of the beacon above them snapping as more oil was added.

"Odd. I'll see you, Husem," the man beside him said, and the youth grimaced. "You're too young to be a gamester, I think."

He had a face gone thick with age and a long scar that ran from his chin up to his ear, just above the line of his jaw on one side. When he grinned, as he was doing now, it had the effect of creating what seemed a double smile on that half of his face.

"He lacks ability," the dealer said.

"Short on talent as well," the man said, to the laughter of everyone but the youth. The others at the table followed through with their bets, all odd.

Masiph id Ezern bit his lip. "I hope this is all above board," he said, staring at the dealer whose hand had strayed back to the cup.

"I hope so too," the man, Achelluth, said. "Someone short on talent and without ability certainly can't handle the underboard of life."

Masiph bit his lip again, not replying, and the dealer pulled the cup away, revealing two dice—a four and a three. There were whoops from around the table, but he did not look up, his eyes fixed on the dull bones whose pips had betrayed him again.

"That's it. I'm out," he said, pushing the last of his coins across the table. "I'm getting some air."

"Neither the coin nor the stamp for it, Husem," Achelluth called out, the white of his scar almost gleaming. "You haven't run through your allowance already, have you?"

"Hardly. I have better things to spend it on than at this table."

"Well, at least you are wise enough to know you will be spending it here," Achelluth said to more laughter. Masiph just nodded and walked out the door.

He wandered from the tower, stopping just outside the glow of the beacon to lean against the ramparts. It had been a cool day, given the rains could not be far away, and now that the sun was nearly set the night brought a chill. One of the two men on patrol on this stretch of the wall passed by, and they greeted each other. Masiph reached into the folds of his robe for the pouch that held his aslyn and put a quid in his cheek.

"Quiet night," he said, as the soldier passed back in the other direction.

"Every cursed night is quiet, Husem."

Masiph smiled, starting to work at the quid, as he stared idly at the veil of the night descending upon the desert. Here, so near the Eresnan River, it was a green desert—the short grass and sage brush that was its hallmark, plentiful and vibrant in color and scent. Once the rains began there would be even more as other plants began to flower. It was something he was curious to see, for though he had lived in Darrhyn his entire life he, like so many others from the city, had not set foot outside the western wall. When he had travelled it had been east into the Ferryen Plains, or down the Eresnan where the desert, so near, was safely kept from sight by the trees that lined its banks. To most Darrhynna, the desert was worthy of no more than a wary glance to the west and a scuff of a boot heel at the earth when talk turned to the Shadow Men.

Masiph had joined the Watch at the beginning of the dry season, five months ago, over his father's objections. For once Ibrazol had relented, though it had not felt like a victory as Masiph had expected. It felt like his father had in some way outmaneuvered him again, achieving his desired end in allowing his son this. Perhaps he had. Masiph never could tell what his father's thoughts were and was still not clear on his own feelings now that he had achieved his desire. The work itself was tedious—a few weeks on, a few days off, and always a quiet night.

This in spite of what one could hear walking the streets. To listen to the talk there was to believe that the Imperial city's very existence was precarious, given its location in that nebulous region near the Empire's border where the desert began. And the desert was the Shadows' domain. Never mind that the Shadow Men, even as they were conquering the desert, shattering the Empire a hundred years ago, had never dared an attack on Darrhyn and its fabled great walls. None had in the five centuries it had served as capital of Renuih.

There had been a raid a week ago in Fardun, little more than a day's journey southeast—the first of the season, and earlier than usual, given the rains had not started. Strangely, the fact that it was an unimportant farming village seemed to lead to even more anguish among the populace. There was no sense to it, but why did there have to be? It was the Shadows, after all. They were without reason and purpose, moving like common beasts with the seasons, content with the barest of existences on the rock and scrub of the desert.

In the streets talk turned to conspiracy and invasion. This was the only tangible result of a Shadow Men raid. That afternoon Masiph had heard that the shadows were gathering near Ghehel and were working to rebuild the Nasuila Bridge to use as a gateway to strike at the heart of the Empire, cutting the Ferryen Plains off from the capital and the southern provinces. At any given moment in the rainy season Darrhyn was a day or hours away from a massive army of the Shadows materializing at its gates. In a week, maybe less, it would all be forgotten—until word of the next attack arrived.

*We live in an age diminished,* Masiph thought, *the shadows of greater days.* Before the fall of the desert, even during that desperate struggle to maintain their hold in that realm, the denizens of this city would never have cowered at the mention of a mere raid by the Shadows. The thought would have been laughable. Now those who had to memorize their invocations, and even some of their betters, spoke of the Shadow Men as the natural inhabitants of the desert. Generations of Renians had known no other life but that of the desert—and that included his own family—yet that seemed to be almost forgotten now, or at least dismissed.

"What's the thought this evening?" Nustef id Illied said to him as he stepped out of the tower. The Nohritai was older than his fellow nobleman, with narrow features and a heavier green tone to his skin than was usual for those from Darrhyn.

"We can only bear a life of fear so long," Masiph said.

"Heavy things indeed, especially for someone with no marrow in his bones," Nustef laughed.

"Where else do you find the pox but in the bones?"

"The voice of experience, perhaps? Are you preparing lines for your chronicle?"

"I don't think so. The historians just put whatever words they want into the mouths of whoever anyway. Husem Azyereh was illiterate, I've been told."

"Really?"

"Yes. He was not a favored cousin."

More laughter. "Fair enough, I suppose. I always forget that he had a life before he became the Ad Eselte's Vazeir."

"Someday though," Masiph said, "we'll have to do something about the shadows or we'll be nothing more than carrion for them to feast on. Better to act now than to be put to the squeak later."

"You shouldn't listen to what you hear in the drinkeries. It only bothers the blood."

"The drink or the talk?" he said.

"I wouldn't know these things. I lead a pious life, as my ancestors and the sage Delth proscribe."

Masiph spat over the wall in response and Nustef smiled. "Talk to Our Most Benevolent One. Don't you have his ear by now?"

"Oh yes, I join him daily for his constitutionals and we discuss all the important matters of the Empire in between verses."

"Does he really go walking about every morning?"

Masiph shrugged. I would be the last to know.

Nustef took his own quid out, putting it in his cheek, and the two of them chewed in silence. There was a small copse near the wall that was filled with dahrrynna birds, the capital's namesake, and their animated calls as they roused themselves for an evening of feasting on insects drowned the air. This was the scene that faced them every night as the sun slipped below the horizon, and that familiarity and the calm that now settled over the day's end was seductive.

Masiph felt strongly about what he said regarding the Shadows. It was an easy thing to be passionate about, given no one was so derelict of their senses as to invade the desert. A byproduct of the restlessness of youth, his father would say in that dismissive tone which burned his ears. That his father, and no doubt that useless philosopher Ad Eselte, frowned upon his views only served to confirm them even more firmly in his mind. Something would have to be done, if only because no one else seemed to think that was the case.

The last Renian force to invade the desert in an attempt to reclaim their birthright had been led by a cousin of his father's, Waleen, ten years before his own birth. Two hundred sons, the flower of the Darrhynna youth, had joined him, dazzled by his speeches calling for a crusade to purify the desert of the black scourge, to resurrect those ancestors lost there and restore the empire whole. The result was predictable: a laughable disaster guided by a mad fool. Most failed to return and those who did were ruined, never to be whole again. Masiph had seen a few of them on visits to other Nohritai homes, balding men who walked about like children, unsure of each step.

Such a catastrophe had the effect of ensuring that no Ad Eselte or Nohritai would propose a war against the Shadow Men for generations. Still, Masiph admired Waleen his madness. His cousin, he thought, probably had felt much as he did the echo in each step of his life. If a cauldron of blood in the desert was necessary to drag this plain into a new age, then let it come.

"He's a poet," he said, breaking their silence. "He has the

pouting lips for squeaking after all. Certainly no stomach for war."

"Probably he's too concerned about self-important Nohritai who think they know better than him how to run the empire." Nustef said.

A clanging bell, not far down the wall, stifled Masiph's reply. They both looked at each other, not quite believing what they were hearing. It was an alarm. Darrhyn, first city of the Empire, was under attack.

# 2

The procession had lost any pretence of cohesion. People milled about drinking and watching various groups of musicians playing the sacred songs while dancers tried to keep time to the stumbling rhythms. Cureders took any opportunity afforded by a lull in the cacophonic orchestra to proclaim their day's sermon. "Be the light" was the ragged cheer that could be heard at the conclusion of any song, followed by some hoarse thoughts frantically put to voice on the need for balance in this disturbed era, before the musicians began anew. A woman, dressed in a mask of feathers dyed scarlet and little else, wandered through the procession, pausing at intervals to point skyward and let loose a curdling screech.

It was the third and final day of the Feast of Balance in Lastl city, and, as with the rest of the Realm of Craitol, the feast days concluded with a parade in honor of the Gods. What was unique in Lastl was the procession leader, which by tradition was a newly shorn ardeh. It all began in the morning at the city gates with Cureders intoning competing invocations throughout the crowd. The city's Gatekeeper led a group of representatives of the leading families of rank to shear the beast, still heavy with its winter wool. They were assisted by the animal's keepers, who worked with quick economy, squatting on the struggling creature and attacking its coat with flashing shears, while the noblemen stood by awkwardly, trying not to get in the way, as some of the more exuberant of the crowd called them ardeh-biters.

As the wool was stripped off, it was carried by the noblemen to

8

a fire of nashen wood and incense to be burned while the Sanader of the city and two of his Cureders chanted prayers to the Gods over it. The shearing complete, the noblemen helped roll the creature over, one of them getting kicked in the head, while the Gatekeeper ended up covered in piss to the delight of the crowd. A slap to its flank sent the ardeh on its way, darting forward with its strange, loping stride through the crowd. Cheers went up as it snorted and bucked, kicking an unfortunate few not paying close enough attention as it went by.

Nobleman and peasant, merchant and porter, mingled on the streets empty of litters for this day, people of all rank and class joining in song and drink. They followed the ardeh the rest of the day, the masked woman still shrieking, though by late afternoon she was reduced to little more than a dry croak. Hawkers went through the crowd offering food and drink and harder stuff, helping to restore the collective's strength.

With the day nearing its close, the crowd started to dissipate, the nobles leaving for celebrations at their estates, or, if they were fortunate in rank or connections, at the Gver's Palace, while commoners drifted off to taverns and music halls. The ardeh was left nosing about the streets for whatever sustenance it could find, with only four men remaining to carry on the procession. They serenaded the beast through the twilight, first with whatever sacreds they knew, then whatever hall songs came to mind, until finally, their bottles drank and their voices hoarse, they ran out of music and drifted off into the night.

•••

All the windows had been thrown open, so the scent of the orange and olive trees outside drifted in on the gathering. A few had taken their cups and were out on the balconies, the better to appreciate the night air and the scents of the seven gardens of Jesieles for which the Gver's Palace was justly famed. The three of them had fallen silent, stirring the wine in their cups, when Ludenn noticed a tall man in soldier's dress passing near the door and called him over.

"Tysaras. Allow me to introduce you to two notables. Sedar, Chair of the Morning of our fair city, and Nes Asnen. Tysaras is a levied officer," he said to the other two, "assigned to the pyrsedies for how long?"

"Two winters. This was my first."

"Clearly a man of influence if you were able to get leave for the feast and an invite to the Palace."

Tysaras laughed. "Lucky in cards, I would say. There were two invitations for the officers. One went to the kehel and the other I won at the seconds' table."

"What was the game?" Asnen said.

"Five-card eycher."

"You sell yourself too short," Sedar said. "Eycher is a game of skill."

"You still need the cards to win, no matter your skill."

"A modest and intelligent officer," Asnen said. "All this time spent with Ludenn I'd forgotten it was possible."

"Just because I prefer to employ my talent in the laugh and liedown does not mean I am unfamiliar with loftier pursuits," Ludenn said with a smile.

"Yes, we know you spend most your days studying in Sedar's academies."

Ludenn shook his head. "Well, if I'd known all I was going to get was mocked, I wouldn't have invited Tysaras to join us. I had him convinced I was a man of respect and influence."

"So tell me," Sedar said, "what's life like in the pyrsedies? One hears such tales."

The young man shrugged. "There's some truth to that I guess, but I haven't found it much of a hardship. There are hard men among the common soldiers, and the laborers are even worse. Really we're more magistery than soldiers out there, keeping the asylums."

"A poor place for an officer to be sent, I guess."

"It depends how you look at it. If you do well they look at you more highly than someone with a softer posting. For someone like myself, whose most influential friend is the illustrious Nes Ludenn...well, I probably have a better chance of advancing there."

"Oh, so this is how it is now," Ludenn said.

A pair of flickers in the tree behind them stirred at their chuckles. "In all honesty though, my young friend does not give himself enough credit. The pyrsedies are awful. The levied soldiers are a poor lot at best, mutinous at worst. All a result of our friend Nes Asnen and his like sending the worst of his that way. To say nothing of the laborers, who are common criminals at best. And the shadows and disease. It is the worst of the Realm. Any officer who acquits himself well there is worthy of honor."

Tysaras nodded in thanks to Ludenn. Asnen leaned against the balcony, "Have you seen much of the Shadow Men while you've been there? We keep hearing the border is quiet, but one wonders what that means."

"We've only had one attack since I've come on. To the south, especially near the coast, there are always more because of the Renian highways and the Republics. But the pyrsedies around us haven't had to deal with much. That may change with summer. I hear they move about the desert more with the rains."

"There was that one attack you had to deal with a month or so ago, wasn't there?" Sedar said to Ludenn.

"Yes, they somehow slipped past the pyrsedies. They were having a grand old time of it in the eastern estates when we came upon them. Almost got ourselves into a bit of trouble on that one, but we made out."

He started into telling Tysaras a story involving himself, Asnen, and three dancers of the Evening, so Sedar excused himself to refill his cup. After the cool of the balcony the heat that met him inside was oppressive. There were no more than a hundred people in the hall, which could easily hold twice that, but the day's warmth and the humid bodies had conspired together unpleasantly. At the far end of the room was a stage where dancers and musicians sought to keep the wavering attention of those nearby. There was a troupe of acrobats to follow, he knew, as well as some actors to conclude the evening with the creation performance.

None of the talent was from the Morning; the Alastl had long been for the Evening and this Gver was no different. He would do well to keep an ear open to see if there was anyone that might be worth buying away from the other faction. The Gver was known for having a discerning ear for musicians, and also for his eye for dancers. If some of the rumors he heard were true, the Evening had to turn over half its dancers every season just to keep the Gver's interest.

He found an attendant who mixed wine and water in his cup and then decided to return to the balcony, although he knew he should be talking with any supporters of the Morning who were here to ensure that all his performers would be busy through the summer.

As he made his way, nodding and smiling at those he knew, a hand grasped his elbow and a woman said, "You've been avoiding me all night, Sedar."

"Not true," he said, turning and smiling. "I've been avoiding the heat."

"Oh, you poor thing," she said, a grin touching her lips. They were painted scarlet to match her silks, bringing out the subtler red of her skin to good effect. She was the wife of Bessu, a city magistrate and a loyal Morning supporter.

"Do you know Nes Rysseh?" she said, gesturing to the small man with owlish eyes at her elbow.

"Rest assured," Rysseh said, "I've been a Morning as long as your husband."

"The Morning owe much of our success to both your families."

"I do hope that we won't be discussing the games," the wife of Bessu said. "I find the whole thing so tiresome."

"There's always time for that."

"What would you care to discuss?" Sedar said to her.

"Nes Rysseh and I were just talking about the rare appearance of the wife of Our Immortal Gver."

She gestured over Sedar's shoulder and he turned and saw Niriese ul Keleprai, surrounded by various ladies of the court, her face pinched and drawn. The conversation around her was animated, but she seemed withdrawn and distracted. Sedar watched with no little fascination as she turned to the woman speaking with a slight, confused smile. He had not, he was quite sure, seen her in over a year, and he regularly attended court functions. In that time he had heard any number of rumours as to her condition: that she had lost the use of limbs, that the ravages of the plague had left her face so horribly scarred that she refused to leave her quarters, or that one of the winter fevers had struck her and left her mad. All apparently untrue.

"Is this the first time she's been in public?"

Rysseh shook his head. "She was with Our Illustrious Keleprai at the Ceremony of Naming."

"I hadn't heard that," the wife of Bessu said.

"I was there. She did not look well. She looks much better tonight."

"Really. She doesn't look at all good to me."

"That day she could barely stand for the ceremony, and she didn't stand at all through the invocation. They carried her in and out on a litter."

Sedar pursed his lips. "You just wonder how long she is for this realm."

They all watched her for a moment, the gauntness of her cheeks, how drained they were of their natural red shade. The severe set of her mouth did nothing to dissuade their impressions.

"I wonder how she can display all the signs of rot and her husband none when the Illustrious Gver spends all his time beneath the arches of the Evening."

"He does take the road well-traveled," Sedar said. "Perhaps his badge has been enseamed with his house's rampant honor."

"That's awful," the wife of Bessu said. "I don't even want to hear any more."

Rysseh smiled and shrugged, meeting Sedar's eyes. "Well then, what would you care to discuss now?"

"Unlike the two of you, I have actual news, not just tawdry rumor. Bessu told me he has it on good authority that Our Most Majestic Qraul Laterala intends to allow Rakai to join the Sea Challenge this summer."

"Now this is news," Rysseh said.

"What brought this on, I wonder?" Sedar said. He had been to the Challenge once with his father and his ten-year-old self had thrilled to the sight of those huge vessels sweeping through Xln harbour. He had not understood what was taking place, the attacks and the feints of the ships, but it had been awe inspiring nonetheless. Especially with the crowd covering the entire docks, far greater than any he had seen at the games, even in the Qraul's Pantheon in Craitol.

"Perhaps our young Qraul has a reformist streak in him?" Rysseh said.

"Is he even allowed his own thoughts?"

"Now, my dear," Rysseh said, "I'm sure both the High Adept and Our Immortal Gver allow him some time for reflection."

"That is probably taken by his Qraulla, though I hear she is more salamander than wolf," Sedar said.

"It would explain why she has not risen yet, I suppose," the wife of Bessu said.

"I would hazard that she requires a heartier broth than that boy provides."

A piercing giggle rose above the chatter of the gathering, leaving an awkward silence in its wake. The talk resumed, though a few amused glances were cast in the direction of the Gatekeeper of the city. He paid them no mind, cackling again at something one of his companions said. Although he had arrived after the dancers had taken the stage, he was already well into cups and was pale and sweating profusely, a sign that he had dabbled in more than a little mythres as well. His companions, all lesser nobility of the second and third ranks, were mocking him loudly, pointing to his sad appearance.

He laughed along with their jests, pouring back more wine as he did, but when he spied Gver Keleprai nearby making his way through the crowd he excused himself.

"Immortal Gver," he called, more loudly than he had intended.

"Noble Gatekeeper," the Gver said.

"Cousin. Brother."

"I would hope, Assyh, that I am one and not both. That would speak ill of my mother."

Assyh giggled loudly again, drawing titters of consternation from those nearby. "Oh. Yes. Cousin. Cousin, of course. I have a request, Most Immortal."

"Indeed."

"Yes, ah. It is, you see, my current office, Most Illustrious."

"Noble and worthy work."

"Oh, indeed, Most Gracious. Indeed. It's not that, of course. The work is, that is to say." He was startled by the loudness of his voice. But the goodwill of the wine rapidly overcame that and he found his way again.

"That is to say, Most Gracious, as much as it is noble work, I would most dearly like. And I feel my talents could be better used. Indeed. In another office, one more befitting of my rank. You see."

"Indeed."

"That is, ah, well, I believe, Most Immortal that, well, the appearance of a relative of the Gver does not reflect well on the office. You see."

"Do I need to remind you, noble cousin, why you were in need of such an unbefitting office?"

This elicited another giggle from Assyh and he fumbled with his cup.

"That is to say," Keleprai added, "I agree that someone of your rank should not be in such an office as Gatekeeper of the city."

Assyh flinched as if he had been struck a blow, his face going flush. "Do you know," he said, "that the cursed ardeh pissed all over me this morning? Some louts were calling me an ardehmonger in front of the whole city."

"These are the hazards of working with livestock, cousin. I'm sure in coming years these duties will weigh less heavily on you. I will take your request under advisement as well. Perhaps in some time I can authorize a review of your performance by the Master of Offices and we can determine whether you are worthy of reassignation. Be the light, noble cousin."

Keleprai nodded and then walked away, leaving the Gatekeeper standing alone, his mouth working silently while he passed his cup from hand to hand.

The dancers and musicians had retired, with acrobats taking their place onstage. Those nearby stomped their feet in encouragement as the troupe began with a routine on stilts involving flaming batons. As if on cue, attendants moved through the crowd with buckets of chipped ice for the celebrants to put in their cups or against their faces. There were several rooms adjoining the hall where couches were laid, along with trays of sweets and cheese. People began to gravitate towards them as if some signal had invisibly passed among them. Others sought places where they might taste some mythres or salen without any watchful eyes. And still others took advantage of the shifting crowd to slip away for more private assignations.

Most stayed in the main room and on its balconies. The acrobats, having doused their flames, were now engaged in a sword-swallowing routine and the crowd around the stage responded with more insistent stomping. A Cureder standing nearby, rattling in the wind, was exhorting his two companions on where he stood in several theological debates of the moment, with one of them playing advocate to his considerable frustration.

"Assuming we are formed in the image of the Gods, as they were formed in the image of the Nameless, then it seems clear that only one of the brothers Melinon drew to her side could have impregnated her, and thus humanity's father had to be either Ulternon or Senteur—but not both, as some would suggest."

"But why," the advocate said, "could the Goddess not be like the female wyle fish, which, as you know, collects the seed of many male wyles to impregnate its eggs? Isn't it said that all creatures were spawned in her loins? Like the wyle fish, we could have theoretically an infinite number of fathers."

"It does not even pass muster," the Cureder said. "One father is the only logical conclusion to draw, for surely the Gods are more alike us than some common, mouth-befouled fish."

It followed then, according to the Cureder, that the next obvious conclusion to draw was that Senteur was the father of us all, for Melinon would have clearly wanted to have a touch of the glory of the heavens in her children.

The advocate responded, with a deepening grin, that Ulternon was likely the chosen, for he was of the earth and the earth provided life, which was what the Goddess wished for her children. Or perhaps she was like those frogs and lizards, who, bereft of a male to mate with, are yet able to produce offspring. Then she might have more the aspect of a worm and have simply cut herself into an unending number of pieces, each of which became a living child. As she was unending herself, there was no need for conservation.

The actors were well into their performance by the time the Gver had finished circulating among his guests with well-wishing and he could allow himself some unwatered wine. He moved away from the stage, where the actors running their lines were competing with shouts from those in the crowd who desired another version, whether for aesthetic or theological reasons. Celebrants murmured and inclined their heads as he walked past and he nodded in turn. He had just decided to head for one of the other rooms for a sweet and perhaps something more when someone began to beckon for him.

"Nes Kigarle Vistuvyr a Nepene," he said as he wandered over.

"Most Sacred and Beneficent Gver," Kigarle said with a bow, "I thank you for gracing us with your presence. I was just informing my illustrious company of the triumphs of your youth."

"And yours as well, naturally," Keleprai said.

There were three others with Kigarle, a friend of the Alastl and his for many years. One was Nes Javiel of the Dyhens, whose father had been at his side ten years ago, along with Kigarle, when the armies had gone north to put down the Kragian uprising. His newly betrothed, Anisse, was beside him. Keleprai had stood for them at the ceremony only two weeks ago. The third was a young noblewoman who he vaguely recognized but could not place. Her hair was swept up, but he could not recall a husband or their families.

"Naturally, Gracious Keleprai," Kigarle said with a sweep of his hand in front of his impressive girth. "Do you know that these children, these sprites, know nothing of the gleaming reputations we possessed in our younger days?"

"Presumably we still do possess them."

"Speak for yourself, I should say."

"I should warn you, Most Immortal, that some of his stories could be considered treasonous," Javiel a Dyhen said with a smile.

"I have no doubt, noble."

"I was just about to tell them about our evening in Senteur's cloister. A fine story, but I thought you should be given the opportunity to defend yourself."

"I have always said it is your foresight I most value, Nes Kigarle."

Kigarle inclined his head in thanks and then turned to his young companions. "It was a summer night, many years ago, still early. A glorious night. There was a half moon, so we could make our way on the side streets without much difficulty. A perfect evening; it had been so hot all day and then the cool was so sweet, it was almost like a taste in the air with the ripening fruit in the trees."

"You are a poet, Nes Kigarle," Anisse said to him, and Keleprai snorted to the amusement of the others.

"But now, to the point," Kigarle said, lowering his voice. "We were in Nrai, a wonderful city if I may say. Why? I really don't remember. The Sea Challenge? I don't think it was that time of year, but perhaps. Noble Keleprai, do you recall?"

Keleprai waved his hand dismissively.

"You see how it is. Do you see? All these long years of faithful service and this is how our noble and gracious Gver deigns to treat me."

"Long years indeed," Keleprai said, and the three youths laughed. The young woman, whose family he still couldn't recall, touched him on the arm as she did, and he smiled at her.

"This discussion will clearly get us nowhere. At any rate, our Most Immortal lord and I, and several others, who will stay nameless for brevity's sake, because each of them has a story as to why they were there and so forth. Now we had been drinking obviously, we were young then, our beards hardly grown in, and a night in Nrai should not be wasted by youth. We had settled nicely into one of the finer public houses then, where the best musicians of the season were playing and various and sundry were about, including many about whom songs would later be written. It was, in short, looking to be an evening to mark. Alas, not to be.

"How can I express my sorrow, and indeed my rage, at what happened? It does not seem possible that we should be pulled from the establishment and into the darkness, but we were. And it was because our Most Immortal Gver was so insistent on the matter and brought it up continually. You see, unlike today, when he forgets things from one moment to the next, his memory had a lamentable persistence.

"It was, there seems, a woman in the city who Most Gracious Keleprai had at one time pursued. Who he was still pursuing. Now, she had been so terrified by his affections that she had hidden herself in one of Senteur's cloisters."

"As I recall, she was a student of astronomy," Keleprai said.

"Or perhaps her father had placed her there to protect her virtue from so scurrilous a youth," Kigarle continued without pause. "It doesn't matter. At any rate, we were treading our way towards holy ground.

"Now she had concealed herself in the cloister, but noble Lastl had some way or another—he had some contact among their Cureders, who knew what was going on, if I remember. So all we had to do was get him in there and whatever would happen, would happen, including, most likely, our eternal damnation. Of course, that would only occur if we were discovered, and Most Gracious Keleprai had a plan. The larger details escape me, and are unimportant really, but it was definitely not Mentirenius stealing into the keep in the dead of night.

"Ah, it comes back to me now. Don't laugh, young man, it will happen to you sooner than you think. We bribed the men on watch for the evening to look the other way as we scaled the walls. Oh, we shall be doomed to wander for eternity outside the doors of Ulternon's Hall for what we did that night. Regardless, we forged on through the various gardens of the place to the main quarters. The three of us were sentinels while Keleprai went in. Everything seemed fine. No one was up for invocations, and we were out of view of the observatory. But then he kept taking longer and longer to return. We started to get concerned. What if he had been discovered? What if the lady had called the guards down upon him? How soon would they be coming for us?

"It took him forever, but just as we were rolling some dice to see who would go up to look for him he came down and we made a graceful exit. All of us we returned to the city, aflush with the daring of our deed, and naturally we wanted the story. He'd spent so long in the room we all knew what had occurred. It seemed quite obvious. But Most Gracious Keleprai wasn't telling, which was most unlike him at the time. People in Kragi Province were versed in the intimate details of his life. Naturally, this only piqued our interest, and we were convinced that this would be the tale by which all tales would be measured. A story to be set to song.

"It took us until the sun was up, and we were all getting understandably a bit disturbed from the lack of sleep, but we got the story out of him. And I repeat it here for you now and insist that it never be forgotten. It seems Gver Keleprai had gone into the building, up the stairs and to the left, as he'd been told. Come right to her door, or at least what was supposed to be her door. He never did find out. Why, you ask, and well you should. Because the priests caught him in the act? No. *Because he never went in.* He spent the better part of the night standing outside the door wondering whether or not he should. As he said, 'I couldn't decide what to do or why I was really even there, and so I just left.'

"Now, I must say we were somewhat appalled by the whole thing and rightly so. We had risked our lives and our immortal souls—and I suppose we shall still see about that—and all for what? For him to stand at the door *and dither.*"

"Was it as he says, Most Illustrious?" the lady asked Keleprai to the laughter of the others, her hand brushing his again.

"He has the larger points more or less as they happened," Keleprai said. "I won't quibble them. I do seem to recall, though, that Nes Kigarle was so far gone by the time we exited the establishment that we practically had to carry him over the wall. Fortunately, he hadn't gained the stature that you see today."

The four laughed loudly, though Kigarle immediately began to protest loudly that he had taken only three glasses of wine on the evening, all judiciously watered, and anyway he wasn't so girthful now.

Another guest, Ussul a Vellar, a cousin of his wife's, pulled him aside and Keleprai resisted a grimace. No doubt, he wanted to ask for the favor of the Gver, just as Assyh had. Ussul was more worthy of honor than his cousin, a ridiculous, drunken fool, but he was still a youth, with little to distinguish him from any other noble of the second rank, beyond his relation to the Gver's wife. As Ussul begged forgiveness for his intrusion, saying that he only wished to speak of a position under the Master of Offices that he felt ideally suited for, Keleprai stared past him, his gaze fixed upon the young woman, who remained with Javiel and Anisse as Kigarle excused himself. She had, he thought, as he feigned interest in what Ussul was saying, the most wonderful eyes, almond-colored and alive. Remembering her touch upon his arm, he decided he would have to make certain to find her again before the evening came to a close.

# 3

Just as the bell started to ring it dropped silent, leaving a dimming tremor of sound in the air, more ominous somehow than the thunderous clang that had preceded it. Masiph and Nustef remained rooted in place, unsure what to do. It still seemed impossible to them that an attack could be underway. The darrhynna continued their chatter, oblivious of this brief disruption to the placid evening, the alluring stillness holding.

Masiph took a step toward the far tower and leaned out on the inner wall, trying to see beyond it. Somehow the last of the light had gone out of the day in those last moments before the bell had sounded and the night was upon them fully. His eyes were drawn to the beacon's flame and not the surrounding darkness. In the space beyond he could discern the mass of the wall, but little more.

There was no sound anywhere. He wondered if he had somehow gone deaf in the moment. A clatter of activity behind them broke the reverie, the others in the quadra rushing out of the tower.

"Why's it stopped ringing?" someone said, his voice sounding strained and high. Masiph could not find a name for the voice, his scroll of his mind blank.

"Where's the patrol?" This was Achelluth, snarling at him.

"They were just here." It seemed he was speaking. "They must be over by the tower."

Everyone began speaking then, their words spilling over each other.

"I don't see them. Does anyone?"

"Maybe they went into the tower or…they went to investigate the bells."

"They're not supposed to leave their posts."

"Where's it coming from? Is there an attack?"

"Do we stay here? Or what?"

Someone was swearing, unleashing a torrent of curses, the same ones over and over.

"Well, Husem," Achelluth said, "you're the one in charge here."

Masiph nodded curtly and turned back to where the bell had been ringing. Was it the tower nearest or one even farther along? He could sense everyone waiting.

"Get the torches. Two of you guard the tower entrance. Send somebody to the other tower," he said, pointing behind them. "Get the boys up in barracks if they're not. And the rest of you spread out along the wall, short patrols. I'll go see where our patrol is here."

Without waiting to see if they would obey his orders, he turned and walked down the wall. The moon had gone behind a cloud but he could see the way without difficulty, the beacon his guiding star. He drew his sword and took his shield from his back. He could hear the others talking as they lit the torches and he cursed under his breath that he hadn't thought to take the time to get one himself or to bring someone with him. He dared not turn back now and risk looking like a fool in front of those who, he suspected, already assumed him to be one. His spear was in the tower as well by the dicing table, though he wasn't sure which weapon he preferred in this situation. Time would tell. Ahead there was only silence, broken by his own footsteps.

Why wasn't anyone else responding? They had to have heard the bell. And why, for that matter, had whoever sounded the bell stopped ringing it? You were not supposed to do that. His mouth was very dry. He ran his tongue along his lips; it felt like a foreign creature moving inside his jaw. He could see it, a thick, multi-segmented insect stepping gingerly down his chin, feelers darting out tentatively. The eyes, massive spheres that covered most of its head, were a dull red.

The patrol was gone, a fact he confirmed when he reached the door to the tower. It sat slightly ajar, light from the beacon leaking out from the sliver of an opening. He paused for a long moment to listen for any sound within. There were indistinguishable noises from all around: his quadra behind him, the barracks being roused. Were these the sounds of an attack in progress? He couldn't say, but within the tower all seemed still. The insect, having retreated into his mouth, was now descending his throat, which twitched at the movement.

Trying to ignore the tickling sensation in his stomach, he stepped forward and pushed at the door with his shield, his sword poised. It was caught on something and he had to put his shoulder to it. It gave with a sudden lurch and there was a shifting of form and weight behind it. He went back on his heels, shrinking behind his shield. The soldier he had spoken with earlier—every cursed night is quiet—spilled over into his path. Masiph was fixated by the odd smile on his face, as though he had been the recipient of a practical joke he found distasteful.

Adrelluh? Nabiv? No, something else.

The sword had entered just below his heart and then been pulled, with a vicious sweep, down and across the body. Haimert? His stomach had been punctured and his robes were soiled with bile and half-digested food.

He dragged his eyes from the corpse to look at the rest of the tower room and saw tables and chairs overturned, with bodies sprawled amongst them all. The smell of blood and piss and innards, a strange and musty stench, corroded the air. Everyone was dead. He looked down and saw that he was standing in blood. The insect was scratching at his stomach, its quivering mandibles grinding against the softness there.

How could he not have seen anything? How could they have heard nothing at all? The door to the stairs that led below to the city was open.

He ignored that for the time being, glancing above to the lookout where the beacon and warning bell were. Another deep breath and he went, sprinting up the wooden steps. In his haste he caught his foot on one and tumbled off the stairs, landing on his shield, his sword flying out of his hand. He scrambled to his feet, bringing his shield up to ward off any blows.

None came—the beacon room was empty but for the body of the man on watch. He was sprawled under the bell rope, his sword not even drawn. Masiph nudged him aside with his foot and began to pull violently at the bell. He continued until he heard someone below. Nustef poked his head up the stairs, his face drawn and white.

"Who did this?" he said.

Masiph did not hear him over the bell's clanging. "Has anybody gone to rouse the barracks?"

Nustef nodded, touching the pommel of his sword. "Yes. I sent Achelluth," he said, and then repeated the question so that Masiph could hear.

"They're in the city," he said, but Nustef looked confused so he yelled it again. Nustef nodded thoughtfully and looked at his feet, touching his sword again.

"Get someone up here to keep ringing this. Send two. We should try to flash the other towers. They're in the city. And there may be more coming."

Masiph did not even notice who it was that Nustef sent up; he simply handed the bell cord over and shouted some orders as he tore down the stairs. He was shocked anew by the devastation below and stopped to look through the open door down the stairway that led to the city. It was not lit, so he could not see to the bottom. He glanced out the other door down the wall and could see his quadra spread along it with torches alight. Farther along, the rest of the Watch had begun to do the same. Standing there, he resolved what his next steps would be.

Before he had time to act, he realized he had forgotten his sword above and returned up the stairs with a bustle of energy. It was only when he arrived at the lookout that he noticed the bell had stopped ringing. The two men who had relieved him were staring at each other dumbly.

"Stop grabbing your cocks and get ringing it," he shouted. He nearly ran into Nustef, who was halfway up the stairs.

"Why did the bell stop?"

Masiph ignored the question. "I'm heading down," he said, gesturing towards the open door. "Everybody else holds position for the barracks."

"Why down there?"

"They aren't about to walk out through the gates, are they?"

Nustef nodded. "No. No, I guess not."

He paused before heading out to the wall. "Who is it?"

Masiph shrugged. "Luessans, maybe. Seems their sort of stupidity. Keep an ear for me above. I may call for someone to join me."

Masiph descended the stairs and then stepped out from the wall to a lamp-lined street, a cluster of buildings immediately across from him. Beyond that were the long, twisting streets of the city, each one seeming to lead to two more. The moon was behind the clouds, leaving the lamps isolated in the obscurity of the darkness. His thoughts rattled around in his head, colliding and failing to coalesce into anything solid. They seemed louder than the bell and the Watch calling out on the wall, all but drowning out the barracks responding to the alarm.

The question was what the attackers were about, and tied to that was who they were. If it were truly a Luessan plot, or indeed the machinations of any of the three kingdoms, then this was likely a small incursion, easily handled. Disruption the intent, rather than anything of real consequence—though he could not imagine why the attack had come from outside the wall when any one of those nations could easily infiltrate the city with their agents. They were Renians after all, even if they no longer recognized the Ad Eselte or the Empire. And if it was the Shadows then ancestors help them all, for there would be more to follow. The thought made him shiver.

There were shouts above him on the wall, which meant the barracks had responded. He was distracted by that, looking down the wall at the tower to see if he could distinguish the forms moving along the ramparts, when what sounded like a scream cut through the night. He leaned forward, straining to hear more, but all he noticed was his own breathing.

It came again, short and muffled, originating in one of the buildings across from him, unmistakeably a cry of terror and pain. He hesitated, knowing he should wait for the rest of the Watch to arrive, and then started towards it, gripping his sword so fiercely the pommel cut into his hand. He was down the street and at the entrance before he had a chance to think any further. The door was open just wide enough for him to slip through. Inside he waited a moment, trying to let his eyes adjust to the shroud. He wondered at how he had again not thought to bring a torch from the guardroom.

It was a merchant's residence by the size of it, someone who owned a shop in one of the inner districts but was not so successful that he could afford a place of this size near there. He wondered if the attackers might be targeting this family, but dismissed it. There was no chance this merchant was important enough to bother with this kind of effort. Whatever the case, only the servants would be sleeping on this level, so he started to make his way to the upper floor.

There was no point in wondering anything, especially what he was doing here, he told himself as he went. It was impossible to see much farther than his hand could reach. He had to feel his way forward, hoping that he didn't run into walls or furniture and that he could find his way from room to room without alerting whoever was already there.

Somehow he made it from the entryway down the hallway to the stairs without incident. It left him exultant as he began his ascent, though that feeling was checked by the fact that he had not heard anything since he had entered the house. Likely it meant that everyone was dead. And that, in turn, meant that the intruder was on his way back to him.

When he could sense that he was near the top of the stairs he took great care with his steps so that no sound would betray him. The silence threatened, his own breathing marking him to the killer who lay in wait somewhere in the shadows. His arm ached from gripping his sword so tightly.

He felt the presence before he saw anything, and even then it was barely discernible, a bit of substance to the air. The intruder came to the same realization a moment later and took a quick step back, his boot heel striking the floor, which reverberated like a thunderclap through their shared silence. Knowing he had to act while he still had surprise to aid him, Masiph took another step to get off the stairs, raising his sword. He was already on the landing though, and his foot came down heavily, striking him off kilter for a moment. He took another step to settle him and put him within striking distance of the intruder, but as he did he felt the blade slide into his stomach.

There was no immediate pain but he could feel the object foreign and somehow cold within him. He was face to face with the intruder, could feel his breath on his face, a stink of meat and unfamiliar spices. The man said something that sounded halfway between surprise and laughter. It was not a Renian word and the accent was unfamiliar, which could mean only one thing.

He gasped, and that seemed to rouse the Shadow Man. It

yanked the sword out from his guts and pushed him back hard with its shield. The world lost its hold and its firmness; somehow his head was below and above his feet. His sword was out of his hands and then his shield too was jarred loose. It hadn't realized he was there. The thought was dumbfounding. There was a tremendous noise, he supposed from his fall, and it seemed to echo louder and louder in his ears.

Had the beast gone or was it still here? He tried unsuccessfully to look around, but his body, sprawled at the bottom of the stairway, did not respond. There were some fleeting seconds of awareness left to him before he slipped from consciousness and the one remaining lucid portion of his brain wondered where all this clumsiness had come from.

# 4

Donier a Fieled, a noble of the third rank, and an officer in the army of Lastl, was not watching Gver Keleprai, as so many others in the palace for the Feast of Balance celebrations discreetly were. He was staring at the woman beside him, who at that moment was laughing at something he said and laying her hand on his arm as she did. He excused himself from his companions so that they did not notice the direction of his gaze. He did not trust his face to hide his emotion, he had taken too much wine. One of the balconies was empty, but for a Cureder and some scholar discussing Senteur's heavens, so he went there, affecting to take some air.

In spite of himself, he turned from his feigned interest in a nearby tree where several sprites sang to watch the woman, Liene ul Terainous a Fusel. She and the Gver were now carrying on their own discussion separate from the other three, his back to Donier while he could see her face. He forced himself to look away at the tree before she noticed.

His rage surprised him. Why should he care that she was holding court with the Gver? It was appalling, but no more so than any number of other transgressions that marked the passing of days. What did it matter who the Gver might turn his attentions to, and that the lady might encourage it as well? That her husband was missing, dead in all likelihood, not even a month ago; well, perhaps she was simply looking to her future as best she could. Still, she would not even be here, would be sitting in her home in a mourning gown, if they had only found Terainous' body. It was odd, he thought, that the Afusel were allowing her about the court given current circumstances, but she was obviously being escorted by the other noble couple who were conversing with Nes Kigarle, and perhaps in this day and age that was all that was required for the sanctity of a woman to be guaranteed.

It had been a nightmare. A small band of the Shadow Men had evaded the notice of the pyrsedies and set about razing and looting the countryside east of Lastl. In response the Gver sent Nes Ludenn and his cohort, including both Terainous and Donier as seconds, to hunt the beasts down. They marched down the old Renian highway for two days before they came upon the still-smoking ruins of a way station, the defiled bodies of the innkeepers and postal men strewn across the road.

The area around the way station was forested, nearly the last trees one would see passing through to the desert. Only the burned-out buildings of the station and the path down to the river were uncovered by foliage. After a cursory investigation of the slaughter, the cohort spread out along the path, most clustered near the river filling their flasks. The Shadow Men materialized from the dense underbrush, as if their dark flesh were formed from the very gloom that lay overgrown there, with swords drawn, shrieking their awful war cries. Everything after was confusion.

The men who had straggled behind on the path to the river were cut down. The five tasked with burying the dead of way station fled down the highway. The rest of them were left to form a poor phalanx, their backs to river, and it wasn't long before Donier found his ankles wet and his foothold slipping. The Shadows snarled and yelped, sensing the desperation that had seized the remaining cohort.

He could not say when the battle turned. There was no singular moment, no coalescing of the disparate spirits gathered, no transformation from the many to the one, which songs and chroniclers always spoke of authoritatively. Looking at it dispassionately, as Donier did these things, it was a matter of superior numbers finally telling the tale, for, though nearly a third of their men were killed in the first moments of the battle, the cohort still counted nearly twice the men.

In the midst of it all, with the situation at its most dire, Terainous was touched—a demon's hand, there was no other explanation. The gossip about it was everywhere. He wondered if Nes Liene had heard any of it. He himself had not, for no one would dare say anything of it to him, but he knew what was being said. And he could deny none of it. He had been there, heard Terainous whooping and shrieking, saw him throw his sword at the beasts as they pressed in. Then he had turned and flung his shield into the water and tried to swim across the river. The waterway was wide, the current quick, and he was pulled downstream. The last any of them heard of him Terainous was singing some child's song from his youth as he floated away.

When the Shadows were routed, half the remaining cohort was sent in pursuit. Ludenn led that group, leaving Donier to cremate their dead. Afterwards, he spent the better part of the day scouring the forest downriver for any sign of his friend until he sensed the men growing restless. They returned to the highway and set off in search of the deserters, laying them to the sword.

Nothing was done after, no party sent downriver to see what trace could be found of the missing second. As far as the Lastl cohorts were concerned, he was dead and there was no use in sending anyone to investigate. Better for everyone to assume he was than to go out and find otherwise. Donier understood their reasoning, but he still felt it was a disgraceful way to treat the heir to an important family. He was a noble of the second rank, after all.

The Afusel had refused to accept the cohort's verdict that Terainous had passed to the Hall, which explained why Liene was not in mourning, and that was surprising in its own way. A family of their stature would be expected to prefer a dead son to the return of one with senses beyond this realm, especially when they had other heirs.

When his emotions had cooled enough that he thought they would no longer show, Donier rejoined the festivities within. The Gver and Liene had disappeared into the crowd and he returned to his companions, resisting the urge to see where they were and what they might be doing.

Her name, Kigarle had told him, was Liene ul Terainous. The Gver still felt he should know who she was, but the names meant nothing to him and he dismissed it. How often was he left with this feeling? Too much these days, he thought ruefully, as he stared intently at her almond-colored eyes. The musicians had taken to the stage again, playing some of their quieter numbers, the romances and the tragedies. The air was finally beginning to cool somewhat as the crowd dwindled and the strains of a breeze passed through from the balconies.

He had contrived to speak to her alone beside the stage, the crowd ebbing and flowing around them. She had been eager to talk to him, he thought. He noted the flush on her cheeks, from the heat or wine. She was watching the musicians intently as they performed and he followed her gaze. Only two of them were playing: one of his court players and a man who, by the pale hue of his skin, was Kragian. They were singing a romance that had been popular before the Northern War, though then it had been played with Mgetir pipes, not the two guitars they were using. He could not remember the last time he had heard it, yet the words rushed back into his mind as if they had always been there for the asking.

"What a lovely song," she breathed as they finished. She was very young—could not have been married for longer than a year or two, he thought.

"Haven't you heard it before?" he asked her. He was aware of others watching them as they stood close. It was her eyes, he decided, the way they turned her whole face alight that made her so enchanting. Her features were plain but the eyes made them dance.

"No," she said. "Is it old, Most Gracious?"

He laughed. "That depends. How old do you think I am?"

Her eyes widened, "Oh, Most Immortal, I didn't mean—"

"I know. I know," he said, laughing again. "But I am old. That song was written just before the war. It was the only song you heard the summer before. And I think I've only heard it a handful of times since."

She turned back to the stage as the musicians began to play again, this time a recent song, one which had been heard in every music hall through the winter. He watched the rise and fall of her dress. The song finished and she turned to him, nervous he thought, considering her word and how to proceed.

He decided not to give her the chance. "You are too young to understand, perhaps, but do you know how a singular beauty can drive a soul to utter distraction?"

She smiled, flushing even more deeply. "You are most gracious, Immortal Gver. I wonder if I might speak to you of my husband." Her voice dropped. "He's been missing, Most Beneficent, since the Shadows' raid last month. There's been no sign of him for good or ill since."

With that, her name was no longer simply a name: *Liene ul Terainous*.

"I wanted to ask, Most Gracious, if it is not too much consideration, if perhaps you could send another party to search for him. It has been so difficult these last weeks, not knowing one way or the other."

He said something, agreeing to speak with Adept Tehh about it later, promising her. Cursed old fool, how could he have forgotten that, he thought, the ground no longer so sure under his feet.

"I cannot imagine how hard it has been. Let us see what we can do to ease your mind of these worries this evening," he said, taking her by the arm to lead her away from the stage, the eyes of the crowd upon them. His eyes were on her, though: how young she was, how light in every movement.

Keleprai spent an hour chasing sleep behind closed eyes, the heat of the wine swelling to distraction within him. It finally chased him outside, where the day's humidity had at last been cast aside for a sweet and pleasing cool. His rooms opened onto a terrace overlooking the city from the tower's pinnacle at the palace's centre. He took an elaborately decorated bowl from one of his bed tables and brought it out with him, placing some of the ground powder in his mouth. The mythres dissolved in a pleasant rush and he followed it with another pinch, setting the bowl on one of the tables that decorated the broad terrace.

There was always a melancholy strain to his thoughts when sleep defied him in the depths of the quiet of the night. The mythres seemed to help, and when it did not, it at least allowed the time to pass more pleasantly. Without it his thoughts became a succession of futility and despair, leaving him with a sensation of being shackled in a stinking pit at the bottom corner of his mind. His captors had forgotten him and there he lay chained, the sunlight never stretching far enough to reach his brow. It was this until the mythres took hold, and, on some truly awful nights, it was this afterwards as well.

He tried not to think. It was best that way, to surrender to the drift and hope a reverie took hold. This evening it did not happen, and instead he found himself thinking about Dalenna again.

Strange, after so many years, to be thinking of events so trivial in the grander scheme of his life.

At the time it had seemed momentous, an illicit affair between two unbetrothed and unpromised youths, he the heir of the ranking Gver, she the sole daughter of one of the most important of the Great Families in the Realm. An overwhelming and all-consuming passion—or so it seemed in those rushed months. They both swore they would defy their families and find a way to marry: some renegade Cureder, a rundown temple in another city where they would need the money and wouldn't ask many questions. It could be done, they said, and made their plans, usually in the warm aftermath of wherever they had sequestered themselves. He declared that he would be with her even if it meant he would never be Gver.

When word came, it was through one of her attendants. She was promised, her wedding would be in half a year's time, to the Qraul of the Realm. She would be Qraulla Dalenna ul Lestulatera. The court in Lastl was inflamed with talk after of the triumph her family had managed in succeeding to place her on the throne. They did not speak again, except officially, when Keleprai had occasion to present himself at the Qraul's court.

He had been devastated and taken to bed for days in utter despair. It was straight out of a forgettable romance. In fact, he wrote several awful retellings of the events himself, though good sense late in the day prevented them ever seeing the light. How ridiculous to think that they, given their families and who they were, could ever dream of having love guide their fate.

It was not youthful passion that drew his mind back to those days, that towering emotion and the feeling that this betrayal would ravage him through to the end of his days. The desire to make every moment larger had grown tiresome long ago. Life had quieter devastations in store, to say nothing of its grim repetitiveness, the way every day was muted by a script already written, his lines in place waiting only to be scanned. He had no idea why thoughts of Dalenna again held his mind in a fevered grip. It was beyond him to study himself in that way, to pierce through the shrouds that lay within. He had never been one to dwell on such things. Those thoughts had never troubled him till lately, and he could not say why that would be.

He noticed a blurred light rising on the streets beyond the walls, a dim and spreading orange afterglow. The beginnings of the sunrise. Dalenna stood within it. Had she been in those shadows all this time? The roof of his mouth was thick and woollen; it was difficult to move his tongue, and he wished he had remembered to bring some water with him. There was a cry from somewhere in the depths of the night—a woman's? Dalenna was smiling and waving at him as she turned and walked away, disappearing around a corner, submerged again into the night.

# 5

A swimming darkness engulfed him. Masiph flailed against it, struggling to rise, but there was nothing solid to hold anywhere and he fell back again and again. He could feel someone watching him from where he lay. He tried to turn and see who, but contort himself as he might he could not lay eyes on them. It seemed the black-skinned thing was above him, staring down, shapeless in the night.

The dim roar of rain pouring somewhere outside reached his ears, startling him. He came back to himself, now aware of an overwhelming thirst, the need made greater by the rush of water coming off the roof above. He could taste blood in his mouth and his throat was raw. Everything hurt, actually. He was awake, he concluded, reasonably enough.

He decided to set out on his way and limped into the streets, which were empty, the night still heavy about them. The rain was driving into the roads, filling them with gorging puddles, overwhelming the gutters. He drank his fill and was soon left soaked and shivering. After wandering for a time it occurred to him that he was looking for someone, whoever it was had been watching him earlier, and he began to walk with greater purpose. The streets, which had seemed familiar, were unknown to him and he was soon turned around and utterly lost.

He stopped in front of a building where the door was open. After looking around he stepped inside with care, glancing over his shoulder to make sure he wasn't being watched. Bodies littered the entryway, some without legs, others missing arms or torsos. He had to step carefully to avoid getting tangled in the entrails that covered the floor.

He noticed Nustef sitting in a chair off to the side and approached him. There was a long gash from his chest down across his stomach. He had both hands on the wound, holding it so that his guts didn't come spilling out. His eyes, Masiph noticed, had been gouged out.

"It's not here," Nustef said, shaking his head and waving one bloody hand toward the door before replacing it fast as he could on his stomach.

Masiph nodded and turned to go. Glancing down, he saw Achelluth's head on the floor. "Husem," the head called out, its lips stretched into a mocking grin, "you have a sodden spirit." Masiph nodded and went outside.

There he thought he saw something at the end of the street, though it was difficult to tell through the rain and darkness. He tried to follow it, turning right as it did, and he found himself in the desert. The heat coming off the scrub and rock was insufferable, and he danced from foot to foot in distress as he tried to see where it had gone. The harsh glare of the sun made seeing anything against the horizon a challenge, but the clouds began to drift in and the rain resumed in earnest. The scrub land didn't turn to mud as he expected; instead the rain vanished below the surface, leaving no trace. But shortly after the very ground he stood on began to stir and bubble as air trapped beneath him was released. Even as the fetid reek of the air stung his nostril, the earth began to dissolve at his feet and he started to sink below.

Masiph's back felt as if he had been dragged along rocks for some miles. He lay still, resting in a pool of his own blood. Stirring at last, he reached down to his stomach to see if his wound had closed, but the pain sent him back into the spinning darkness. He had forgotten that his arm was broken. Using his other hand, he started to trace the wound and found that it had grown. Edging his fingers inside, he was startled by the emptiness. No liver, no stomach, no intestines. He went farther down and encountered a gooey mass slick with blood and other liquid, not quite at his groin but nearing it.

It was almost too awful to contemplate so he pulled his arm

out, wiping it clean across his breast on his Craitolian silks. His heartbeat was a dim flicker at his fingertips. The sun was directly overhead, bright and uncovered, making it difficult to open his eyes, but he forced himself to, hoping for a distraction from the terrifying vision of the gaping hole in his stomach that would not leave his mind.

The desert lay around him, its wide empty sky above. He could smell the native flowers come to bloom with the rains. Mixed among them was the stink of spiced meat. There seemed to be a mountain sitting on his forehead, its weight distracting. He heard the flowers whisper beside him, and turned to see it approaching again to feed.

Water dripped into his mouth, gathering in its crevices until he managed to swallow. Masiph tried to open his eyes, but shut them, the sun overwhelming, pinpointed directly at his head. Someone had their arm around him, holding him up into a semblance of a seated position. He turned to see who this person was, the water dribbling down his cheek instead of into his mouth. His eyes failed him, though—all he could discern were fraying colors, red and green and black. Coalescing shadows. A voice murmured something he couldn't understand and an adjustment took place so that his head lay back and water again entered his mouth. He coughed feebly and shivered. The sunlight seemed to be burning a hole in his head, but it didn't last.

# 6

The ship arrived at Hessen not long before daybreak. The pier was already busy with fishermen heading out on their morning runs and another trading vessel in the midst of being loaded. Word went down the dock to the trading company that their vessel had arrived from Craitol, and a work crew began to straggle in to unload the silks that were in the hold. The captain wandered off the ship, leaving the first officer in charge of unloading the cargo and headed into the city for the company house. A Craitolian left with him, which drew a few glances from various onlookers, the more so because he was of Kragian extraction by the shade of his skin. They walked together to the end of the pier and then parted, the Craitolian heading to the Custom House that lay just outside the city walls.

Vyissan was ecstatic to be on land again, his feet firm about him. Sailors, he knew, spoke of being too long at sea in that weary way everyone has speaking of a burden they alone must carry, one they cannot live without, but they were thinking in terms of weeks and months and port after port. For Vyissan, one day was too long at sea—his stomach never steadied, his balance never became sure. This had been the first time aboard a vessel since his journey south to Craitol over four years ago, an experience he had sworn never to repeat. His was not a lot in life where he could make such vows.

Not helping to ease the difficulty of his voyage had been the captain of the vessel, a foul Nrain. He had distrusted Vyissan from the first instant, the peninsulars always suspicious of northerners, especially one with his shade. Two days into their journey from Nrai he had asked, through his second, that Vyissan not eat with the other officers. He was free to eat with the common sailors or on his own. No reason was given him, though the second to his credit had been embarrassed to deliver the message. Vyissan had not made an issue of it, taking his meals in his quarters. In his circumstances he did not need attention drawn to himself.

For all the frigidness of their passage, their parting on the docks of Hessen was a warm one; the captain glad to be rid of this particular burden and Vyissan relieved simply to be back aground. He was not yet free of his own burden, hidden in the satchel he wore across his shoulder, an unremarkable weight though it yoked him as tightly as any beast, and would not be for some time yet. In fact, he would hardly have time to wash the taste of this voyage from his mouth before he would begin another. But he would not think on any of that now, with his equilibrium regained he determined to slake his thirst and find what women were on offer in the city. There was a brothel district not far from the port, far better in quality than the harlots one would find outside the city walls, which the second officer had given him directions to. When the clerks in the Custom House had read over his letters and gone through his belongings to their satisfaction he made his way there, his steps growing more sure as he went.

He took a room at one of the academies and had the first untroubled sleep of his journey. On the vessel his dreams had been shadowed by the task set before him. He carried something with the power to reorder their profane realm, if those who led him were to be believed. Such a thing could not rest easily on the mind, and his nights had been filled again with images that had dominated his childhood night terrors: the Council Adepts scouring Desecrators, alkemya ravaging their minds and souls, leaving them ruined husks of men. Vyissan could remember the Adepts and their Craitolian soldiers going from home to home in the Fegh district where he had grown up looking for those who had stood with Kercubegahedd against the Council. At the time he could not fathom how they could know that his cousin, hidden in the straw of their roof, was there or that he was an insurrectionist. That he had learned later.

When he emerged the next morning he had altered his appearance. His skin was now the olive-green hue of those of the east rather than his normal sallow color. This, combined with his silk and ardeh wool robes, gave him the look of an Enir merchant from any of the city states that lined the desert coast. A man of no real consequence—or so he hoped. He walked out without receiving so much as a glance from the madam or the swords she had keeping an eye on the entrance. Later in the day someone wondered what had become of the Craitolian northerner who had taken a room the night before and one of the servants was dispatched to see what was keeping him, for the girl had not even spent the night and he had not called for another or for food. The room was empty but for the ash from his burned letters, and there were a few comments about how strange it was that a Kragian could leave unnoticed. His room and the girl had been paid for, though, so no one gave him much thought.

He made his way back to the docks to find a ship sailing for Sylaron, the Renian city that lay at the mouth of the Rensnan. From there he planned to find a boat heading up river to Darrhyn. He fervently hoped that river travel agreed with him more than sea or the next few weeks would be an unending misery.

Hessen was a quiet port, its trade mostly with the nearby Republican cities, so there was only one vessel he could find heading to Sylaron, and it was not due to leave for three days. It was a Renian company, as he had expected, which suited him well. An Enir entering Renuih on a Renian vessel would not attract questions, and in his position questions were what he had to avoid. He had heard any number of stories of Craitolian merchants being turned back at the Custom House in Sylaron, or worse, imprisoned or enslaved. Who was to say what the veracity of those tales was, but it seemed wise not to tempt the Gods' hands. The last thing he could afford was a close search of his satchel, that would truly get him killed. Gods forbid they somehow determined he had knowledge of alkemya, which they might if they searched him— that was punishable by death in these realms.

The second led him aboard the ship for an inspection, sounding its merits as he went. Vyissan nodded politely, thinking that even if the boat were overrun by vermin and all its crew stank of pestilence he would still take his passage.

"You'll not lack for companionship," the second told him as he led him below decks to the passenger quarters. "We've another passenger with us. He'll share the quarters with you.

"And perhaps his own quarters too, if tales of their kind be true," he whispered to Vyissan, adding in a louder voice, "He's here now. You can meet him and gain the lie of the land, as it were."

The second ducked in through the doorway of the fore deck quarters and pulled aside a hammock to allow Vyissan an encompassing look. There was a man stretched out in another hammock, and as he levered out of it and came forward with an offered palm Vyissan had to stifle a gasp.

"Hello," the man said, his Enir heavily accented with his native Kragian tongue. He held Vyissan's arm a long pause, staring into his eyes, Vyissan praying to the Gods that none of the thoughts flooding his brain were showing on his face.

Of all the cursed luck, to be on a ship with Nesyur Geshlvyr a Fegh. A Kragian, from Fegh. Their families had known each other in passing, though Vyissan doubted Nesyur would remember him. The Geshlvyr were a family of low rank, which passed for something in Fegh, while Vyissan's family had no rank and only modest means. He had still been a boy when Nesyur had gone into exile. The years had not been kind, but there was no doubt of who it was.

"So you are to be my company, are you?" he said, releasing his hand and smiling again. "My name is Nesyur."

"Atasem," Vyissan said, forcing a smile to his face. "I am considering the vessel."

"It is quality, quality as you can see," the second said, thrusting his face between them.

"Not much choice either, as I'm sure you've found."

"No," Vyissan said. *Nesyur.* It was beyond belief. He had to remind himself that he was still in disguise and that his accent was holding firm. The Gods mocked all, those who pretended to control their destinies especially, but *Nesyur.* The name was a curse in the right company in Kragi. In Craitol too, for that matter.

During the alkemycal war between the Council Adepts and Kercubegahedd's rebels, every northerner was forced to swear fealty to someone. There was no standing apart, now or then— enough blood had been spilt on both sides that no one's hands could remain unstained. It had been a war over the very soul and practice of alkemya and a war for the freedom of Kragi. The Adepts had called the rebels Desecrators of the Balance for their alkemyc engines, and for daring to defy the Council and its proclamations. The rebels had decreed that the slavery of the Council and the Qraul could stand no more.

In a war of true believers, Nesyur Geshlvyr was something else entirely. He had received Council training, though he had not been talented enough to be inducted into the ranks of Adept and Disciple, and when the first stirrings of the insurrection were heard in Usgelt and Asder he had insinuated himself among the rebels, sending regular reports to the Adept in Devew on what was occurring there. When it later emerged that the Adept and his Disciple were using the alkemycal engines of the Desecrators, Nesyur was implicated in turning them from the Council. Even as they were being executed, Nesyur was ensuring the capture of the rebels who had supplied the engines to them. Following that, neither side could say for certain whether he was working for their interests, and so both turned against him. He had fled the province, barely escaping, and had not been seen in over ten years.

And now here he was in Hessen on his way to Sylaron.

"What would take a Kragian to Renuih?" Vyissan said.

Nesyur smiled. "That is a tale in itself, not a happy one at that, so I'll not burden you with it."

It was a simple mistake and the second seemed not to notice it. There had been no change to Nesyur's expression either, but Vyissan was certain he would be aware of it. How could he not? Someone from the Republics would have called him a northerner. That Vyissan had called him by his kind, even in the Enir tongue, could only mean he was from Craitol.

Vyissan smiled in turn, disguising the rising turmoil within, and carried the conversation to safer territory, commenting on how beautiful a city Hessen was.

"It is one of the finer Republics I have seen," the second said, and Nesyur nodded. "And the academies. I'd a ramp my last time through so beautiful I'd be a brother starling with any man, with a dozen men, for the rest of my time if it were in her nest."

"What is your town?" Nesyur asked Vyissan. "I cannot tell from your accent."

"Tuissar." One of the more populous Republics, and the man who had taught him the Renian tongue and the Enir dialect had been from there. It had seemed the safest choice at the time; he could easily adopt his tutor's accent and the city was large enough that he could navigate most conversations without exposing the true depths of his knowledge. Nothing was safe just now, though—it was only a matter of time before he made another mistake. Nesyur would be sure to press him, to confirm what he now suspected.

"A marvelous city," the second declared, his eye still on the coin.

"Grand Republic. I spent two years there." *Of course.* Vyissan had to resist shaking his head.

"There is a square there—the name escapes me now. It was between the Hezier's Palace and the silk market. The gesht would gather there in the evenings and sing, and all the old men. As perfect a square as exists in our earthly realm."

"A marvelous square," Vyissan agreed.

"Strange to say it reminded me of home."

Now, what did that mean? Vyissan raised an eyebrow as if to inquire, feeling his breath go still in his chest.

Nesyur gestured as though the sensation could not be captured by mere words, so feeble and devious, "It was only…I grew up in a town called Fegh, and the old men would all gather at sundown in the squares and play cards and dice and drink. As they do everywhere, of course. When I was a child that was where I would go. And when I was in Tuissar, that was where I would go."

Vyissan frantically parsed his words for some metaphor, some meaning that he had buried within that only a Craitolian could unearth. If there was any hidden import it was more carefully entombed than a Renian. He allowed a small measure of hope to seep into his body. Perhaps Nesyur hadn't noticed a thing. It was only a matter of time if he went on this voyage, though. Only a matter of time.

"They also have the best dala in Tuissar," the second said.

"Extraordinary," Nesyur said, and Vyissan murmured in agreement. "Although the cups I had here—"

There was an angry shout from above deck, a name sounded as a curse. The second winced hearing it and nodded at both men before going above.

Nesyur continued, "The cups I had here were unlike any I've ever had. Have you—"

He did not finish his sentence. Vyissan had been waiting until he heard the second's footsteps joining the others above them. Once they did he moved, lunging at Nesyur, the dagger in his hand emerging smoothly from his robes to be buried to the hilt in the other's chest. Nesyur gasped in surprise, raising his hands to ward off the blow too late.

"Whoreson."

Vyissan did not give him time to say anything further, yanking his blade out and grabbing Nesyur, stepping behind him as he did so, and cutting his throat with a vicious pull of the dagger. He was careful to keep his robes away from the blood that sprang forth as he lowered the Kragian into one of the hammocks.

"That blood is only a small payment on what you owe. The rest you'll give in Ulternon's Hall." Said in Kragian, nothing more. Let him wonder who, in the end, had found him.

Vyissan moved quickly, arranging the body on the hammock as best he could so that someone just passing by the quarters might not see anything amiss, and then wiped his hands clean. Nesyur was still in his death throes as he left, blood filling up his mouth and spilling out as he tried to speak, his eyes blinking furiously and seeing nothing. Vyissan went above deck, finding the second and giving his leave, promising to return tomorrow with his decision on the passage.

The journey from the ship across the wharf and to the city seemed to pass in another sort of time, not the steady trickle of accumulation he was used to, but one where drop after drop fell at uneven intervals, and the moments in between the beads passed with all the realms gone still. At any moment he expected to hear a cry rising from the vessel, the sound of running men coming towards him, the summoning of the authorities. None of which occurred. He passed into the city, unable to resist a glance back, and set about on a winding path towards its center.

# 7

Masiph was thinking about Esyln, or what had once been Esyln: the jewel of the desert, now a bygone place, a memory of when Renuih had been an empire in more than just name. It had fallen and the rest of the desert provinces had followed soon after. What were they with Esyln sacked and in ruins? Eslyn held for four years against the Shadows' depredations and the rest of the provinces only another six, the traitorous Enir having long abandoned the empire for their Republics. In ten years, four hundred were undone, unraveled like so much ardeh wool.

Of course, Esyln was not the true Esyln. Masiph knew his history. The original town lay ten miles south. The story went that a merchant had wandered off what was then the northern highway in search of some escaped ardehs that he was planning on trading in Yessel, at the time the only town of significance in the north of the true desert. He found the ardehs in a huge grove of willow trees drinking from a spring and thought it a splendid place for a settlement.

Wells were dug and a town established that quickly grew in size, so much so that in ten years the Ad Eselte sent his soldiers to lay the foundations for what would be the city walls. Sitting as it did, midway between Darrhyn and the western cities on the desert's edge, Esyln was set to become a nexus of trade and commerce, especially because the water from its wells was, by all accounts, limitless.

But less than ten years later they went dry in a matter of weeks. One day the waters could be heard rushing in the cisterns below and the next there was only a trickle, then a dribble and then nothing at all. Panic seized everyone and the populace rioted, overrunning the merchant houses and nearly seizing the administrator's estate. The Imperial army was brought in from Yessel and they began to move people to other cities and towns across the desert, while Adepts were sent in to investigate what had caused the water to disappear.

They found water not far to the north, water as limitless as had been in the town previously, and it was agreed that Esyln should be reconstituted there. They also found that a spiteful trull, a witch in fact, who had been scorned by one of the city's finer merchants, had cursed the town, turning the water away so that none reached the wells. She was brought back to the abandoned settlement, her meddling hands cut off and thrown down one of the wells, and there she was left to her fate and ancestors' grace.

That was when Renuih had still been in possession of the knowledge of alkemya, when Adepts held the ears of Emperors. Now it was lost, just as the desert was. Just as well, some would say, for the Empire was a better place without those unnatural arts being practiced. Masiph was pondering this, not sure where his thoughts were going, before he even realized he was awake. And then he wasn't.

The rain fell in a steady patter, broken every so often by a crescendo of drops that echoed throughout the room. Masiph listened to their ebb and flow. Now that the rains had arrived they could expect these showers each afternoon, sometimes into the evening, for the next five months. The Erensan would swell, along with the canals within the city walls, and the flies would become insufferable. That sound signaled the arrival of misery—at least to Masiph, who disliked the rains and the humidity. At the moment, though, he longed to be immersed in the downpour, to see the clouds above and feel the stickiness of the humidity on his skin.

Anything to escape the confines of this bed and his quarters. It was eating at his resolve, turning his blood.

"Don't you have a wife? She is probably broad-awake at home and you abroad at another's bed," he said to the figure sprawled in one of the sitting chairs, one foot resting on a stool.

The figure stirred. "I'm on leave today, actually, and she sent me on my way."

"And the best you can think to spend the day is sitting here waiting for me to get up. It's a wonder she doesn't suspect me of building in her nest."

"I warn you she is more cuckold than cuckqueen. If you give her the horns, she has the spirit to use them to strike a blow."

"I'm sure she could blow a sound note on any instrument at hand."

"Fortunately, there is only one she has learned the fingerings," Nustef said with a smile. "So I have no fear of leaving her to her own devices. Besides, I did promise Husem Isiran that I would make sure you didn't wander anywhere."

Masiph swore loudly and Nustef laughed. "It's for your own good, you know. At least it'll get him off your back for a day or two."

"Quackery is what it is. Have you listened to any of his nonsense that he's spouting at me? He wants me to write poetry. Bad enough I'm stuck in here."

"Surely you have at least a quatrain in you."

Masiph snorted and turned to the window, which looked down on one of the estate's gardens. He could just see the dome of the family's mausoleum peeking behind the grove of orange trees that his grandfather had planted as his legacy to the Ad Ezern estate. In his mind he could see the entire temple and the path that led to its corner, crossing over the stream that wound through all the gardens fed by the Aesen canal which passed through their district.

He had lain insensible for two weeks, his body wracked with sweats and fevers from the infection in the wound. The healers had been so concerned they had summoned the Ceinobytes to call on his ancestors to guide him to their realm in the upper plains. Then, for what reason only his ancestors knew, the fever broke and the infection came down. Within a week he emerged from his delirium and took his first steps from bed.

Now, a week later, he had nearly recovered. There was still some weakness in his step, and he had to be careful when he sat up or down that his wound wasn't strained, but these were trivial concerns. There was no need for him to be confined to his bed. Probably better that he be moving about—it would help regain his strength. That was why it was so infuriating that Ctuellen and the healer Isiran, an insufferable man, continued to insist that he remain abed, watching him constantly to make sure that he did.

Sighing, Masiph leaned back to his pillow, wincing a bit as he did. "Anything interesting happening?"

Nustef shrugged. "Inspections, inspections, and yet more inspections. We don't see the Corenedor for months and now he's stopping by every other day."

"Those kind always make sure to be familiar with the higher officers. No use spoiling ones goods with the riper classes, you know."

"Oh, I'm sure he's untied his hose and will let anyone over it so long as he can keep his post. He'd open the gates to the Shadow Men if they'd do the same, I imagine."

"Kept to be kept. Do you know, I couldn't even tell you his name."

"Ad Uselled. Once the family of the Imperial Vazeirs, if I'm not mistaken."

"Yes, that's right. And now a Corenedor in the Watch."

"His brother, or maybe it's his uncle, is an administrator, near Inlyehr, along the coast there."

"Ah," Masiph said. "The family outcast, then. I can sympathize. I wonder if he has a cousin who will inherit everything as well."

The healer Isiran barged into the room in a brusque clamor, fumbling about in the large leather pouch  all healers carried on their backs with one hand, the other precariously clenching a pitcher of water.

"Marvelous. You're awake, I see. Wonderful. I've brought some water," the healer said, placing it on the bed stand. "Would you like some now?"

Masiph declined. "I'll be along later. To apply the poultices."

He paused and glanced over the bed table, clucking his tongue in disapproval. "I see the pages I left are still blank. Ancestors know, an ordered mind is essential. For the healing process. It would do you well not to have yourself festering over the wound. It weakens the blood."

He did not wait for a reply, already on his way out the door. "And before I forget. Your father was by earlier this morning. Thought it best not to wake you. He asked that I tell you: the Emperor has summoned you for an audience. When you are well enough. Naturally. A great honor. Something for the mind as well."

The door shut with a thud nearly as loud as the healer's entrance. Masiph shook his head and Nustef smiled.

"I don't know. He's a bit muddled, I suppose, but he seems a decent sort."

"I wonder why," Masiph said.

"Perhaps you are to be honored for your bravery. Stranger things have happened."

"Not many."

Nustef noted an edge to the other's tone and decided to keep his counsel. In the days since Masiph's fever had broken he had come nearly every afternoon before going for his turn on the wall. The first time had been three days after the raid when his friend was still crippled by the fevers, thinking that might be his only opportunity to pay his respects. He came a few more times in the next fortnight and once the fevers lifted, the eunuch Ctuellen sent word to him, asking if he might be able to come regularly to sit with his Jetthir.

"It will be good for him to see another face, Husem," the eunuch told him. "Ancestors know he gets tired of mine when he has free reign. I can only imagine how he feels now. And you are one of his few friends who Husem Ibrazol has respect for."

It still shocked him that Masiph's father, the Imperial Vazeir, was aware of his existence. He was not familiar with high Nohritai manners and customs to know for certain whether or not that had been a request or an order, so he had decided to err on the side of caution and attend to the Ezern everyday. And it was an effort, no doubt, for Masiph was both forbidden and unable to do much of anything but lie there. He slept often, and when he was not asleep he was most often miserable.

It worried him to see his friend like this. He was not whole, no matter his protestations. Not in mind or body. The body looked as though it would heal, but could the soul as well? The blood stirred did not easily return to its native state.

"Husem Isiran tells me you are recovering quickly, though," he ventured, hoping that some of the clouds had passed. "You may not have to wait long to find out what the audience is all about."

"That is what they always say. How do they know how fast any one person can recover?"

"I suppose they don't," Nustef said. "I suppose they look at the average sort."

"Oh they have an answer for everything I'm sure. They had Ceinobytes in to prepare my passing, yet when I recover it is perfectly explainable and all due to their work."

Masiph winced as he spoke, knowing how he sounded. It seemed that he was now always a moment away from either despair or rage, sometimes both, all without reason or warning. It was confounding and he was left uneasy with himself, unsure of how any interaction would proceed. The self he had taken for granted had disappeared, leaving a jumbled collection of pieces with the faint sense of a whole that should be there but somehow no longer existed. Perhaps, as in some of the dreams that had haunted his fever-ridden days, he had eaten of himself, his blood having turned with the disease and his flesh becoming succulent to his ravenous soul.

It was not the attack which haunted; he had barely given it a passing thought since his recovery from the fevers. He had little recollection of it. There were a few scattered images that he struggled to cobble together into some semblance of a narrative: the placid evening along the wall, the guardhouse, the impenetrable darkness of the stairway. In his mind he stood continually poised to take that final step.

"All this sitting is making my blood fester," he said, striking out at the quiet that had descended with Nustef watching him, trying to mask his concern.

"Yes, well, he and Ctuellen are working very hard to care for you."

Masiph nodded, surrendering. "Yes. Yes, they are."

Nustef stood, stretching a bit. "Well, I think I'd better brave the rain. I've been asked to attend at market."

Masiph nodded and turned back to the window, looking past the rain to the mausoleum dome. Nustef hesitated in the doorway, opening his mouth to say something further before deciding against it, and then turned and left. Masiph did not notice, his mind on the rains, thinking about the Ezern paradise Asieren where the family would often retreat for the early part of the season when the storms were at their worst. Would any of the Nohritai be going to their spring paradises this year, or had that all changed with the attack? Perhaps everything had changed. How could it not have? The Shadow Men had attacked Darrhyn. The force of that thought hit him in a way it had not before and he felt his chest tighten. He had no idea what kind of world lay beyond these rooms awaiting his return.

# 8

Vyissan managed to lose his way twice before finding the stairway, tucked into the crook of an obscure street to the north of the Hezier's Palace. He wondered if he had somehow misunderstood the proprietor of the drinkery, for the road was nearly empty of traffic, though it was close to midday and most of the city seemed to be about. The other end of the stairway spilled out into a large market, an extravaganza of noise and color. There were stacks of cages filled with squawking birds and monkeys and the air was heavy with the stench of their refuse mingled with roasted meat being turned on spits. He saw fruits he did not recognize and skins of desert snakes.

There were a few mercenaries gathered around a statue that, as he had been told, was missing the left arm. He told them what he wanted and was met with hard stares as the swords tried to gauge what he was about.

"Why not take a ship to Sylaron?" one of them said, a Renian judging by his shaven face. "Why risk the desert road?"

"Is it so great a risk?" he asked them. "Surely it must be used."

"Not so often by those that can afford to hire swords to go with them."

"Why take the risk?" the Renian agreed.

Why indeed. Vyissan resisted a rueful smile. After wandering the city for most of the morning to ensure that his trail had been well and truly lost, he had settled into a drinkery for a cup and a seat where he could observe the comings and goings on the street while he mulled his predicament. In the end it seemed wise to leave the city. He thought it likely that he could avoid arrest—little good it would do, for the docks were now closed to him. The second and the others on the vessel would have supplied the authorities with a detailed description and the wharf would undoubtedly be where they would concentrate their search, given it would be known he had been trying to get to Sylaron. Removing his disguise was one option, but then he risked being ensnared by Imperial agents once he arrived in Renuih.

He had considered and then rejected heading west to Besar, the nearest city, a day's walk and still within the Republic, or Erphem two days beyond. Besar was unlikely to have a vessel that did not pass through Hessen, but Erphem certainly would. The old Imperial highway, though, was notorious and little used, and there was the fact that he would be traveling in the wrong direction given his ultimate destination. If he were to risk the highway, why not try to the east, where nothing but desert and the Shadows lay and then Sylaron? Time pressed him at this juncture, his journey only begun and already threatening to unravel. He could manage some coin to contract some swords for the journey. And why not, why not.

"The next ship does not leave for three days," he said, looking from face to face. "It is three days by ship to Sylaron, no?"

"More or less," one of them said.

"And four days by foot."

"You would save a day or two if you left tomorrow," a man with thick scar across one eye nodded.

"Assuming you're not attacked."

"That day is very important to me," Vyissan said. "Important enough for me to risk the desert road."

There was a silence as they considered this. It was the Renian who addressed him, the others clearly deferring to him.

"What will you be carrying?"

"Only what you see now."

This drew a raised eyebrow. "I am not bringing anything to trade in Sylaron, it is just important that I be there."

"In four days."

"Sooner if possible," Vyissan said. "I will leave this afternoon, as soon as we can gather provisions, provided some of you are willing to come with me."

The Renian studied him and Vyissan met his gaze. Finally the mercenary nodded, as if Vyissan had passed some sort of trial.

"It's no matter to me, I guess, why you want to do this. And if we are carrying nothing of value, all the better. Nothing to weigh us down."

That was not true, but Vyissan agreed. "I will need three of you. Four armed men should make people think twice. I would prefer men who know the road. You do?"

The Renian nodded. "I walked it my first time coming here. I'll go. More work in Sylaron likely."

Vyissan looked at the others and two came forward. They all stepped away from the rest and bartered on price. When they had agreed, they went to a notary who was sitting bored under a tarp on the edge of the square and had him draw up a contract, which Vyissan signed, giving the name Atasem den Adessel. He had the notary read them the letter of introduction to the lending house in Sylaron where he could draw on the money to pay their contract. The three swords gave an X and he clasped each of their palms to finalize the agreement.

It was only once they were outside the walls and up into the hills of red earth and stone that overlooked the city and the bay that the hard-wrought tension that had seized him from his first steps off the vessel, after his murder of Nesyur, slacked in his veins. He had to draw his hands into his robes to hide their trembling. As the road crested the final hill, the city disappearing from their view, Vyissan turned to look to the west. The sun was setting, glorious ribbons of red and gold streaming across the horizon, which from their vantage point looked endless. It almost seemed, if he stared long enough, that he would see Craitol. His life lay elsewhere, though, and he turned to make his way towards it.

# TWO:

# THE DEMON'S WAIL

# 9

Keleprai had not slept again. Had stumbled blearily through the morning, his head aching, as he wondered what could possibly be wrong with him. Just old, he told himself, probably just too godsforsaken old.

That he had to spend his morning presiding over another ball game had not helped his state of mind. It was Evening against Morning, or was it perhaps Midday? He had never cared for sport, and the internecine squabbling of the three factions and their connections to various rivals of his family did nothing to endear them. More importantly on this day, the game did not help set him at ease, which he needed after a night without sleep, followed by word of a coming audience with the High Adept of Craitol.

This would not be an official visit for Cepedutherupt; no one but his Master of Offices would know he was coming. It was Nasyren who had in fact brought the High Adept's missive to Keleprai as he ate breakfast, offering the coded letter without comment, for he knew the Gver would be displeased. Keleprai was always unhappy when word came from the High Adept, for Cepedutherupt seemed to thrive on the internecine and the secret, forever insisting that their correspondence be encoded, their meetings in secret. No matter that no meeting in this palace could be entirely secret. Arrangements had to be made, servants told they could not enter certain rooms, guards assigned to stations they were not normally, all of which served notice to those who watched for such things. There were many who did.

It was exhausting to see to and Keleprai was in no mood to dwell on it that morning, or to think of what crisis of the Realm was upon them now that the High Adept had to travel to Lastl to speak with him rather than entrust what needed to be said to letters. Something of grave concern, there could be no doubt, to risk his being seen in Lastl. There were enough who believed the High Adept and the Gver of Lastl ruled the Realm together that they did not want to give the stories more credence than they deserved.

The last point of the day was scored and Keleprai rose from his seat to applaud. Players from both factions approached the grandstand and the Gver's box, paying obeisance to him and he blessed them in turn. That done he left the pantheon, before the athletes even had time to leave the field of play, his guard barely able to keep up with his pace. People knelt before him as he passed by, but he hardly noticed them, his mind on the High Adept and the troubles of the Realm.

His inclination in these matters was always to do nothing, to avoid the problem at hand in the hopes that it would resolve itself of its own accord. In many affairs this was a sound and just approach, in others things tended to fester and sore. That was what had occurred ten years ago when he and the High Adept had first had occasion to form their alliance to stand behind a young Qraul.

It had seemed at the time a laughable insurrection led by a disaffected Disciple, cast out and forgotten by the Council of Adepts years before. Every decade or so an uprising would occur in Kragi province, usually led by some third-rank noble with delusions of restoring northern rule, or, more rarely, freeing the Kragians from whatever imagined yoke they suffered under. No one in any of the southern courts paid any mind as word came south that a few towns near the Orgrat Wastelands border had gone over to the insurrectionists. The Gver, unable to control his own territory, had requested that the Council send an Adept to deal with the rebels and everyone presumed that would be the end of it.

When word came two years later that Usgelt had fallen and the nobility of all ranks, those who had not escaped or turncoated, had been put to the sword, it became clear that this was not some minor uprising. Many of the lesser northern nobility joined the rogue Disciple's flag, as well as any number of those previously ostracized by the Council. Still, none of the great northern families went over and Fegh and Devew stood, not even remotely under threat. It was a northern problem, for the Great Families there to handle.

It was the Council, led by High Adept Cepedutherupt, who insisted otherwise. Kercubegahedd had to be stopped, they said, and those who had joined him utterly destroyed for the false craft they practiced. Keleprai never entirely understood the reasons for the Council's aversion to Kercubegahedd and his ilk, but he saw an opportunity for the Alastl to become first among the Great Families of the Realm with an alliance with the Council and the Qraul. New to the throne, Qraul Lestulatera wanted to solidify his standing and he insisted that all the families of rank submit forces and that all the Gvers should attend the battle personally. There were objections from all quarters, but in the end they three had their way and that spring the armies went north through Haigah with the intent of catching the insurrectionists off guard before campaign season had truly begun.

They did not, word having reached Kercubegahedd of the approaching force long before they emerged from the mountains to Kragi province. Even still, the outcome was never really in doubt, for while the rebels' force was larger than expected, filled with banners of the minor Kragian nobility, it in no way matched that gathered under the flag of the Qraul. The battle of the alkemyas was more tenuous, though, and Kercubegahedd's forces held strongly for two days, but on midday of the third their line broke and by that evening it was over.

In the weeks that followed they pursued the routed force across the ends of the province. The lands of those who had stood against the Realm were seized, and entire families put to death as an example. The bodies of the guilty were left to rot on the city walls of Usgelt, Fegh, and elsewhere as an example to any northerners who might feel the pull of sedition in their blood. It was never a bad idea to remind the Kragians of the price that would be exacted for their disobedience—they were an unruly lot.

The disaster of it all was that Lestulatera perished in the battle, early on the second day. Keleprai did not see it, but the Qraul and his quadra broke through the enemy lines, near where Kercubegahedd had assembled his renegade Disciples and their alkemyc engines. These were turned on the Qraul, immolating both he and his standard, nearly turning the whole battle in a moment.

It was the death of the Qraul at the hands of the Desecrators that led to the scouring, as the Adepts of the Council referred to it, of all those who had mastered Kercubegahedd's alkemyc engines. In the entire history of the Council, stretching back over the centuries to the beginnings of the Realm itself, only once before had an Adept murdered a Qraul. It went against all the Council taught, was a violation of the Gods' given balance of the Realm. That some fallen Disciple, practicing a black alkemya, was the one to commit the act only worsened the desecration. It could not be allowed to stand; a price had to be exacted to restore the Realm to balance.

Sometimes it seemed to Keleprai that it had to have been longer than ten years since Haigah—it felt like something out of a distant past, a story told him by some wizened relative on a feast day. The Realm had changed so irrevocably in the aftermath of that struggle that it rendered the world before unrecognizable. And yet the specific recollections had a habit of leaping forth from his subconscious with the immediacy of events that had happened only days before.

The smell, for some reason, was always foremost. It had been the late days of spring when they went north, but winter held long in Kragi that year and they emerged from the mountains to a realm in the last throes of the melt. It was the unmistakable smell of a new year, the green just beginning to creep forth from every particle of earth. Later, by the third day, that mingled with the stench of death as the bodies littering the plain warmed in the sun.

The rest was a collection of moments, flashes of things, now connected by the workings of his memory decreeing order where there had been none. Those three days it had felt as though he were moving outside of time, outside of all existence. There were times when he sensed the whole of the battlefield, that churning mass of mud and bodies where the future was being determined, but mostly he was aware only of the immediate struggle before him in all its numbing repetition. Sleep had been easy then, now it was not, and that marked the passing days as much as anything.

That Cepedutherupt had not changed at all in the time since that spring while time had worked its ravages on him was a source of no small jealousy on Keleprai's part. Better to think of that anyway than those final hours of the battle when the two of them had avenged themselves for the death of their Qraul,

Cepedutherupt, and the other Council Adepts immolating Kercubegahedd and turning his alkemyc engines on his followers, while Keleprai led the force pursuing those who fled leaving a stream of blood in his wake across Kragi Province into the Wastelands.

As he returned to the palace and the rituals and duties that were his daily affairs now, Keleprai was filled with a sudden trepidation, and he made a silent invocation to the Gods that he be spared anything resembling those days again. He feared he would not, for he knew the High Adept would experience no such foreboding and would not hesitate to see blood spilled to meet his ends.

# 10

They left the road to make camp, heading to the top of a ridge where there was a grouping of three or four trees that would provide a modest shelter against the desert elements. It was like being atop the rim of the world there, they could see for miles in every direction. Vyissan squinted, looking back along the snaking road where they had come that day, almost expecting to see the walls of Hessen sitting at the edge of this valley. Instead there were just empty waves of air caught in the glare of the sun.

The road was in good condition and they had passed quickly from Hessen up into the hills that divided the coast from the desert, and from there had descended into a broad valley from which they had only just emerged. He did not know enough of the history of the Empire to remember how long it had been since its collapse, but he assumed it had been well over a century since the Renuih had held the desert and this road had been in common use.

Vyissan had never seen the desert before—the nearest he had come was Lastl. The vastness startled him. He spied mountains to the north and was told they were almost two days' walk away. From where he stood now he could see that what he had thought was a ridge on the northern edge of the valley was in fact but a small hill and somewhere in the vague distance he thought he could see a further uprising that might mark the valley's edge. The only creatures they encountered that day were birds, motes in the huge expanse of the sky overhead.

The trees were not tall as they were in the north where he had been born, but instead bent and warped, as if they had grown old right in the bloom of youth. They were surrounded by the clumps of brush that never reached above his knees and seemed to spring up from the earth at random. These were hard plants with sharp, dark leaves and thorn-marked stems. The ground itself was a dull brown, leeched of both moisture and color and thick with stone and dust. Cacti lurched from the earth at odd angles, some creeping along close to the ground, others standing as tall as the trees.

Inahan, the Renian, and Hethuin set about collecting brush for a fire while he and Gessul saw to the food. They had proven themselves competent men from the start, especially Inahan. He had taken command of the two other swords before they had even left the city, and Vyissan had no doubt that the Renian would do the same with him should the situation demand it. There had been little chatter once they left the city walls—the two Enir had talked with each other a bit throughout the day and Vyissan had joined them in a chew, but Inahan had not spoken at all, his eyes always scanning the horizon.

It had been the same at the market in Hessen. Vyissan sent the other two to buy food and supplies while he had Inahan take him to a smithy he trusted, and there he bought a sword to go with the dagger he had concealed in his robes. *There are no spare words in this man*, Vyissan had thought as he watched Inahan barter with the smithy over the price. He suspected he would grow used to the sound of the wind and their footsteps, for that was all he had heard for long stretches that day, or be driven mad by it.

While they had idled in Hessen waiting for the Enir to return to the square with their supplies, a slaver arrived with four of his wares. Three were tribal men, from north of the Empire, Inahan had told him, and the last was a Kragian. Vyissan struggled not to betray his fascination with his brother of the shade. Of course, he knew that Craitolians had once sold his kind, in the time before their conquest. But that had been a hundred and fifty years ago. How long had this man's ancestors been enslaved? It had never occurred to him, though of course it should have, that women had been taken as well as men, and that naturally there would have been families, such as they were. He studied the man as much as he dared, hoping the Renian was paying no mind, and saw that from his features he must have some tribal blood in him or something of the like.

There but for the laughter of the Gods, he had told himself, though the words sounded hollow to him.

They kept the fire low that evening so as not to attract notice, and one of them stood apart on watch as the dusk grew heavier. Inahan took the first shift on watch and Vyissan idled around the fire after their meal with the Enir. He asked them if they had taken the road before, and both said no.

"I've met a few who have, though," Hethuin told him. "Criminals and the like, mostly."

Vyissan ignored the questioning look he gave.

"It's the Maroons you have to worry about," Hethuin added, "or so they tell me. Not so much the Shadows here, though of course you can never be sure."

"How was it?" he called to the Renian standing watch.

Inahan was silent, peering into the surrounding darkness, his back to them. "It was no easy thing," he said at last. Vyissan nodded in turn, thinking instead about his pale brethren escaped from their bonds and scratching out whatever feeble existence they could manage here on the desert's edge with the other Maroons. What kind of life might it be?

# 11

Since his release from his confinement two days before, nothing had felt right to Masiph. It was small things mostly, the sort that before might have passed without notice. The light seemed, not brighter, but sharper somehow. Even within the estate he felt like a small craft attempting to navigate a vast ocean wandering those familiar halls. Everything looked slightly out of focus and he had an alternating sense that things were closer or farther than they seemed. The feeling heightened when he was out on the streets, leaving him almost dizzy.

It was late in the morning, the day green and bright with the unspilling foliage of the trees that lined Isinan, the main avenue that passed through Uenam District south to the Imperial Palace and the mausoleum. The street was flooded with people about their business and he moved uneasily among them, stepping with care, as though a wrong stride might drag him into a swirling tempest.

There was a group of Nohritai youth just ahead of him, separated only by a older woman carrying a bundle of wood unsteadily on her back, and he listened to them jest back and forth with much laughter and insult, calling to the drabs on the street to ask what the market price was. He envied them, their day of idleness. They would have woken late, perhaps only just, gathering at one estate house or another before setting out for the day. It might be that they were heading to an eatery for a late breakfast, and then from there to the Academy, or perhaps one of the other academies, less illustrious by far, that lay in the darker corners of the city. A few weeks ago he might have been among them.

His stomach stirred a bit at the thought of food. He had been so anxious about his impending audience with the Ad Eselte he had unable to eat. His nerves hadn't steadied any since, he had simply transferred the locus of his unease to the teeming streets of the capital. It was an assault to the senses at every turn, especially on the Isinan. There was the stench and braying of ardehs, their keepers yelling as they sought to encourage the plodding beasts to drag whatever load they had been yoked to. The competing calls of the street vendors overwhelmed even that. Their stalls were scattered everywhere, so that the avenue became a warren of smaller byways that had to be negotiated by all and sundry. The crowds pressed in on him from all sides, people everywhere and from all lands. There were Renians from all the provinces and the three kingdoms, with a few Enir mixed in as well, their heavily bearded faces providing a marked contrast to their clean-shaven brethren. He even passed a tribal man, his face and neck inscribed with ritual scars, shouting at a confused vendor in his strange tongue.

He stopped at a table stacked high with ripe-smelling fruit—oranges, mangoes, and pineapples. Flies buzzed around in ecstasy as a man hacked open a melon with a machete, while his wife took various pieces and put them into bowls, sprinkling them with ground chilies and a twist of lime before handing them to customers. Masiph took one and managed to gulp down about half its contents before his stomach began to quiver again. He handed the remainder to a child beggar at his feet who was pulling at his robes. The child shoveled the feast into his mouth, as fast as he could manage, his cheeks bulging monstrously, snarling at two other children who had materialized from the crowd at the sight of Masiph's generosity. One of them tried to seize the bowl, but the vendor shouted at them and brandished his machete, so they all fled down the street, leaving it empty on the ground.

The heat was growing more insistent as the day approached noon, though the clouds that would bring the afternoon's rain had already begun to gather overhead. He was sweating and a bit thirsty in spite of the fruit. The remains of his wound itched with the moisture. The scar ran from his chest down, uncomfortably close to his groin. It seemed impossible that he could have survived just looking at it. Had he not seen the others, split from top to bottom, their guts poured out around them? And yet he, in spite of several weeks' ministration from the healers, had survived. Ancestors provide.

His arrival at the walls of the Imperial Palace, the innermost of the five great walls of the city, brought a great sense of relief at his impending escape from the crowds. The herald announced him at the gates, and, after an Imperial Ceinobyte anointed and blessed him with incense, he passed into the outer courtyard. He was led by a courtier along one of the paths to the gates of the inner wall. The courtier nattered on in a good-natured tone as they went, though Masiph missed most of it, consumed again by dread at what awaited him in the Palace. The courtier paid no mind, continuing to tell Masiph of his arrival in Dahrryn from Inlyehr six months ago, where his family was connected somehow to the Vazeir of that province. Masiph murmured politely whenever the courtier would pause for breath, which seemed to be all the goodwill the man needed to keep the momentum of his tale.

The six blue domes of the Imperial Palace loomed overhead as they came to the inner wall and imperial sanctum, their size almost oppressive when viewed this closely. Again a herald announced him and a Ceinobyte blessed him as he passed through the gates and went on to the palace itself. He was led inside through the main doors, which, by tradition, stood open, and from there he was lost as the courtier took him down hallway after hallway, through one door after another, ending their wandering at a bath where eunuch attendants stripped him and ten others of their robes, washing and shaving them. His hair was trimmed and he was rubbed down with oil before being bathed in incense yet again.

As they were dressing him, the courtier reappeared to take him on his way and he resumed his telling. He had left off with his disembarkation from the riverboat that had carried him from Sylaron to the capital, so he proceeded with an elucidation of his copious impressions of the First City. They entered a great hall, teeming with activity. At its far end was a doorway, before which a severe-looking man stood guard, looking out on the straggling line that extended almost to the other end. There was a steady volume of chatter, made smaller by the sheer dimensions of the space they were in.

The courtier returned, having gone forward to speak with the frowning Gatekeeper, and continued his story. He had presented himself at the palace and was now preparing to spend his first night in his new quarters in one of the buildings in the outer courtyard. As he had settled in bed that first night a spider had come up through the covers and bitten him on the arm, just above the elbow. It was an arangela spider, a bright red thing about the size of a child's hand. The courtier had been unaware that one of the necessary habits of anyone living near the Resnan during the early rains, when the creatures took to wandering looking for mates, was to conduct a thorough search of the bedroom before going to sleep. His arm had swelled up three times its normal size, the bite mark turning an ugly purple and leaking white pus. There were fevers and aches as well, days in and out of consciousness. For a time it seemed he might lose his arm, but before any rot set in the swelling went down and he recovered.

The line moved forward at a deliberate pace, no one here important enough to take much of the Ad Eselte's time. Masiph seemed to be saying something to the courtier, telling a story. He listened to himself, confused. Phrases from those around entered his hearing as well, becoming intermingled with what he was saying so that he couldn't quite get the sense of it. Did the courtier know about his own wound? Was that why he had told his story? He could smell the sweat of the man in front of him.

"When I give you the word, you will step forward to the herald. He will announce you," the gatekeeper said, not even bothering to glance up from the papers he clutched in his hand. Masiph nodded as though he understood, not betraying the overwhelming sense of confusion he suddenly felt.

"Then you will take six paces forward, halt and go to your knee. You will count to six—S L O W L Y—and then you will rise and go another twenty-four paces. Halt again and prostrate yourself fully. His Benevolence will indicate when you should rise."

Masiph badly needed a drink of some kind. The courtier seemed to have gone somewhere and the Gatekeeper had forgotten he was even present, his gaze focused on those still to come. There was a rumble of noise coming from the court, perhaps laughter. His hands felt heavy at his sides, as if they should be doing something instead of hanging there useless. He stared forward at the curtain obscuring the entrance to the court, trying to ease his breathing.

The courtier returned and at his side was another man wearing the colours of the Imperial Vazeir who bowed informally to Masiph.

"Your father wishes for you to carry the Ad Ezern sword for your audience with His Graciousness," the man said, extending the bejeweled scabbard to him. The pommel was a deep red that did not glitter, but instead seemed to draw light within. Masiph unstrapped his own ceremonial sword and exchanged it. Had he ever held this? Perhaps as a child.

"I will meet you after your audience," the Vazeir's man said, bowing again. Masiph was still struggling with the belt, trying to set it about his waist right, the weight of it strange at his side, when the gatekeeper called "Forward" in a demanding voice.

After a moment's pause and a furious glare he went, remembering to keep his pace stately. Two trumpeters sounded as he entered the hall, startling him. He saw the herald before him and came to a halt, staring straight ahead at nothing. On either side of him were generals, ambassadors, and other dignitaries, the companions of the court—and beyond, on a dais, sat the Emperor upon his throne. He could feel all their eyes upon him.

Masiph stood for what seemed like hours, exhausted from the tension coursing through him. When the chorus had concluded the herald turned and declared to the assembled throng, "Masiph id Ezern den Ibrazol, Jetthir of the Watch, Fifth Rank, Protector of this City."

Another silence and then he stepped forward six paces and went to his knee, making sure to keep his eyes on the burgundy carpet that extended up to the dais, running like some polluted artery through both halls and perhaps beyond. He could smell his sweat rising underneath the sweetness of the oil, festering as his whole body clenched and he struggled to breathe steadily. He felt a hint of restlessness in those around him, as if he had stayed at his knee too long, so he stood and went twenty-four further paces before prostrating himself fully.

He imagined himself dissolving entirely into this dirty stream, his sundry parts drifting through that sickly matter, drawn to what heart he did not know. A cry of "Rise, Protector" reached him and he stood awkwardly, his whole body seeming larger than he remembered it. He was abreast the front rank of companions, perhaps twenty paces from the stairs to the dais on which the Ad Eselte sat impassive, staring above them all out of the room at the whole of his domain. Between them, in that empty space that marked the barrier between their universes, were laid the gifts of this day's supplicants. Among them were two cages, one containing two monkeys each about the size of a large cat, their hair black, except at its fringes where it was a heavy green. The other held a leopard that paced the short length of its cage, not one of the larger varieties, but a rarer kind, found only in the deepest of the northern jungles, its stripes red.

"Approach, Protector," came the next cry from the stiff man standing just behind the throne. Masiph walked forward, climbing the dais to its middle step and then stood nervously, unsure where he should be looking. The Emperor rose from his throne, his expression distant and controlled, his hands before him in a gesture of welcoming. He was slender, with thin fingers, and his receding hair, long gone gray, lent him a bookish air that clashed with the stern authority of his expression. Masiph bowed deeply and the Emperor returned his greeting with a nod and a fleeting, empty smile.

"Masiph den Ibrazol, I have followed your career with some interest," he said in a quiet voice. Masiph could hear everyone behind him leaning forward in the hopes of hearing what was said. "Ad Ezern have sacrificed much in the service of this empire, and you are no different."

"Thank you, Most Gracious," Masiph said, not looking into his eyes. He was afraid to move in case he started trembling. He had a sudden vision of himself overwhelmed by convulsions, falling to his knees on these stairs, a jumbled mess, and then, without warning, simply disintegrating, his intestines and feces smearing the walls and splattering the ceiling, his one arm landing near the cage of the leopard who gnawed on it while the monkeys played with his eyeballs.

"I've been told much of your bravery that terrible night when this sanctuary was breached," the Emperor added. "Your superiors tell me you performed your duties admirably." A pause. "More than admirably, in point of fact."

Masiph did not reply. None of it seemed addressed to him anyway. He was a part in a mosaic already laid upon a ceiling to be glanced at by the passing horde.

"For this great service, and recognizing the great history of Ad Ezern in service to this empire and its ancestors, I feel some

71

reward is due."

He stepped back and gestured for Masiph to kneel. "Present your sword, Protector," the crier said. On one knee Masiph held his sword aloft across his head, just above his line of vision.

The Emperor had a vial of oil in his hand and he poured a few drops onto the tip of the blade before taking it in his hands, their fingers brushing as he did so. *I have touched the Emperor*, Masiph said to himself. The tip of the sword touched his head and he shivered as the oil, cool and scentless, dripped into his hair.

"May you honor your ancestors as your brothers so valiantly did," the Emperor said for his ears alone. The sword was removed from his head and the Emperor and the crier sounded in unison to those assembled: "Rise, Suliher."

His ears rang from the shouts of the companions and the sounding of the trumpets. The family sword was in his hands again, though he didn't remember the Ad Eselte having given it to him. He fumbled at his side to place it in scabbard. The Emperor smiled at him again, already looking past him down the carpet to where the herald stood ready to announce the next supplicant. Another functionary stood below him, having appeared from somewhere, waiting to lead him out.

He walked dazed behind the man, past the leopard and the monkeys, which had begun screeching with the noise of the crowd. The assembled had quietened again and turned towards the herald before he had even left the room. Outside the Vazeir's man awaited him, and he exchanged the brightly jeweled sword for his more pedestrian implement. The courtier stood behind, waiting to lead him out.

# 12

The first creature they encountered, excepting the birds passing overhead, was a snake stretched out across the highway basking in the sun. Gessul killed it and that evening he and Hethuin gutted it. Vyissan watched as they carefully extracted the venom pouches connected to the fangs. That completed, they prepared what meat was contained in the creature, leaving only the skin to dry by the fire. As Gessul cooked the snake meat, Hethuin took the venom pouches and made a wide circle around their campsite, dripping the poison on the ground. When Vyissan asked Inahan what that was about, he was told, "Tolote."

The tolote was the second creature they had encountered while resting in the shade of one of the infrequent trees they passed along the road. Vyissan was the first to see it moving at a lope, low in the distance, a dark spot against the late afternoon sun. It looked like a smallish dog, though even at that distance he could see that its ears were much larger. The tail, which he saw as it turned and began to move parallel with them, was long as well.

He pointed it out to the rest, and the two Enir responded by making warding signs. They all watched as it moved to the east, disappearing beyond the horizon. Later, once they were underway again, Vyissan asked the Renian if he knew why the Enir feared the creature.

"They think it is the Shadow Men's familiar."

"Ahhhh," Vyissan said, as though he had heard of such a superstition before.

"Do you?" he had asked Inahan.

"It was ours once," was the reply. "When we had the knowing of alkemya."

The words chilled Vyissan, though they were said without emotion. He wondered what these men might do if they knew what and who was in their midst—would the coins promised them at journey's end be enough to still their swords?

The snake meat was not tough as he had expected, and he enjoyed it a great deal. As he lay down to sleep later, the fire only dim coals, Vyissan saw Nesyur's face behind his closed eyes, his expression locked in that moment of surprise and incomprehension as he saw the knife coming for him. What did it mean, that look? Had he been caught unawares or had he not at all grasped who Vyissan was? One of the others around the fire shifted and he started, a knife coming for him, flashing at the periphery of his vision. He opened his eyes to the night, the stars and moon filling the vast sky with Senteur's distant light. As he stared up at them, unwilling to close his eyes again just yet, he heard the high and mournful call of a tolote somewhere to the east. A moment later there was another, this one more distant and from the north.

After a day and a half, Vyissan's endurance for the quiet and stillness of the desert had reached its breaking point and he attempted to engage Inahan in conversation. The two Enir did not trust him and would not speak to him except to answer his questions. The only words Inahan had spoken were in answer to Vyissan's questions as well, but he suspected that was more out of a preference for silence than any particular aversion. And in truth he was fascinated by the man, the respect the others granted him, and the way he carried himself, hinting at someone who was no mere sword for hire. Vyissan had no doubt this was the case, for he had noticed him reading the contract as the notary wrote it out.

"Did you take the road during the same season the last time?" he asked, thinking, if nothing else they could talk about the weather. The two Enir were behind them, one of them singing in a dull voice. Inahan scanned the horizon with restless eyes and Vyissan wondered for a moment if he was not going to reply.

"No. It was after the rains."

He did not so much as glance over at him, and Vyissan resisted the urge to sigh.

"You are not what you appear," Inahan said after a pause, catching him off guard.

Vyissan looked at him from the corner of his eye as they walked. Inahan still had not broken his gaze from the horizon. He wondered if the others were listening, but Gessul was still singing.

"How do you mean?"

"I know of no merchant who would willingly take this road," Inahan said.

"If it means anything, I have the same feeling about you."

He sensed the shrug without even seeing it. "No sword is what they appear, generally speaking. We are like the ramps beneath the arches with a dozen stories as to how our honors were cracked."

"I suppose," Vyissan said.

A sudden gust of wind howled across the plain, striking them full in the face and was followed by a small whirlwind that spun towards them, forming out of nothing. They were momentarily caught in its swirl, a place of wind and dust, before it spun away and out of existence. Vyissan coughed and spat, his eyes and mouth filled with grit.

Inahan laughed. "Did you never leave Tuissar? Or do you enjoy the taste of dirt?"

"I did not spend much time in the desert, or outside the city for that matter," Vyissan admitted. "And now my lot seems to be the sea more than the land."

Inahan appeared to accept this, grinning and shaking his head slightly. After a time he said, "You're not a merchant and you're not from Tuissar. I would put coin to that."

Vyissan swallowed, still tasting the dust in his throat. "Yet here you are. In spite of that."

"Here I am."

"You are from Sylaron?" Vyissan asked, voicing a suspicion that had been lurking in his mind from the moment the Renian had agreed to join him.

Inahan nodded, and Vyissan thought he saw a grin play at his lips. "Coming up on ten years now since I left. And I haven't been back."

"And that was when you walked to Hessen."

"Oh yes. And now I'm going back."

"Now you're going back. And I am going there too, as far away from my home as I can be."

"There is always somewhere farther."

"Yes," Vyissan agreed. I just hope there is somewhere far enough."

"Time is the only distance I know of to matter."

"Ten years is a long time."

He shook his head. "It may be that I am a fool."

"There is not much choice in anything we do," Vyissan said. "In the end you are left with what you are."

# 13

Masiph had no recollection of having done so, but he found himself in the Darrhyna Market, that mass of stalls and tortuous byways near the Ad Eselte Mausoleum on Isinan down from the Imperial Palace. He had left the Ad Ezern estate late in the morning, wanting to take some air and escape what he felt was an oppressive atmosphere with everyone still fussing over him as though he remained an invalid. Somehow he had arrived here, though he could not remember from where or for what reason. His mouth was dry and bitter with the taste of vomit, and he was drenched in sweat. What he needed, he thought, in what seemed his first coherent thought in some time, was to sit down.

Along with the blue domes of the Imperial Palace, and the walls of the city itself, the Market was what Darrhyn was known for. Viewed from without it appeared vast—within the storm of its daily tumult, as Masiph now was, it seemed infinite. In the Empire's early days, the desert newly claimed, the Ad Eselte had determined to build a vaulted street between the Imperial Palace and the Mausoleum. The corruption of what had been intended as a sacred space had begun almost immediately as transient vendors appeared through the corridor, selling food and trinkets to the pilgrims who had come to worship at the tombs of the past Emperors. The Imperial Guard alternated between tolerating their presence and expelling them, but as the years passed the vendors inevitably became a fixture of the street.

A gradual tranformation took place as carts were replaced by stalls and stalls became shops, in front of which other stalls were set up, that in turn became permanent fixtures themselves. The end result was a warren of stalls and buildings of various states of permanence, spilling out into the uncovered streets beyond. It was often said that the Market was its own law, and it did seem as though the governing forces of all realms were suspended beneath its vaulted sky.

Masiph had no sense of what time it was, though daylight still flooded in through the windows in the high ceiling above them. He could see in the near distance the arches that led to the dark and majestic Imperial Mausoleum. The crowd passed around him in a blur of shifting faces, color and shadow flashing in quick succession. The air was sticky with moisture, thick in his nostrils, the smell of rain, now passed with the sun sharp in the windows, carried in from above.

He realized he was attracting stares from those in the stalls nearest him, so he forced himself to walk on. The smell of chicken on a grill from one of the larger stalls drew him. A group of builders huddled in the dim gloom beneath a ragged tarp that delineated the borders that the proprietor claimed, all of them covered in a thin film of gray dust. They carried on loudly, bursting into laughter every few moments as they gobbled their food. The stall served chicken, along with a bean and pepper stew dumped into the center of the dark, round tulla bread. Rolled up, it was passed to him, the bean mixture oozing out onto his fingers.

It tasted foul, mixed with the vomit and dread that stained the insides of his mouth, but he forced it down his throat, and then followed it with a cup of beer, which did nothing to steady his stomach. He paid and walked away, losing himself in the labyrinth of intermingled stalls. It was its own metropolis, a tumult of alleyways, ramshackle and impermanent. It seemed there were eyes peering from behind tumbledown walls or tarps at every corner. The unease that was thick on the inside of his mouth worsened, and he had the unsettling feeling that he was sinking through the stone of the street.

"So, Husem," Achelluth said to him, his voice insinuating as always. "A jetthir in the army, a real soldier now. No need to fetch mettle for you, now you have the Ad Eselte's proof. You can cast in whatever drab mold you so desire."

The dizziness continued to waft in the recesses of his mind, in spite of the food he had eaten. He propelled himself forward vainly, as if simple locomotion would help dispel the sensation.

"What a reward, Husem, for your glorious courage that night. Surely you deserve it."

What would his quadra think once they heard, which they inevitably must, even though he did not want to tell them? *They will think my father did this. He got me into the Watch, and the first opportunity that presented itself he got me out and into an office that, while still embarrassing, was not entirely beneath the family name.*

Not quite befitting the son of the Imperial Vazeir, but that was easily fixed with time and promotion through the ranks. They remembered that night, they would look at him and remember the truth that yet remained elusive to him. The ceremony had felt like the gilding of a lie, a stained artifice.

"I do hope you will still come to see us," Achelluth said. "Your honor and your example will furnish much treasure, and why should we not be the ones to mine it? Have no fear, I'm sure your gentleman usher will stand sentinel."

He was worthy now of the Ezern name, the Emperor had declared it so, whatever Ibrazol might think. All he had done was nearly get himself killed, failing to save anyone in that house where they had found him. It had been a pointless effort, for hordes of the Shadows hadn't followed that first wave. Only a few dozen had come, and all were found within the vicinity of the breach and easily dealt with. The Imperial Guard had been sent into the streets the following two days, while he had begun his recovery, to seek out any who might have somehow escaped. They found no sign of any further Shadow Men. There had been a frenzy of speculation among the populace and a riot in one quarter, but the capital returned to normal soon after, when it became clear there were no attacks to follow. By season's end it might be forgotten—just another of the strange happenings that seemed to consume the city for a time each year.

As he was walking he realized that he had somehow gotten himself turned around in the Market and was now heading back towards the palace, which some reason made him tremble with fear. More importantly, he now recognized where he was, and after some negotiation of the byways and throngs he managed to find an exit from the vaulted street, emerging from a small portal to sunlight and a near-empty plaza. Once it had been a way station for

Imperial caravans, where they held fairs and traded the goods they had found at the far-flung edges of the empire. But with the loss of those edges, and so much more, the caravans had become fewer and smaller, and now they had their own market outside the city walls near docks where they could trade with the merchants who plied the river.

He started north, intending to return home and gather himself, skirting around the plaza. Nearly halfway along the eastern edge of the square was a platform where executions and other public sentences were carried out by the Market authorities. It was only when he was abreast of it that he noticed the cage sitting at its front, nearly the same size as the one he had seen holding the panther in the court. He gave it a glance as he passed and it took him a few more steps before he realized what was held within, and he had to hold himself from running as he came back. Sprawled at the bottom of cage was a Shadow. It smelled of urine and feces and the festering of death. It did not stir as he knelt before it, though he could see its chest moving slightly. After a time he saw it blink its eyes.

He fought the urge to reach through the bars. No sense soiling himself. It looked as though it were in some sort of trance, and he imagined its spirit not trapped in this place but cast far from the present, perhaps to the west and whatever passed for this vagrant's home. Did this fatherless thing have ancestors awaiting its arrival, ready to guide it through those next endless days? Were its brothers wailing in mourning as they screamed when attacking? He stared into eyes that were vacant and directionless, a growing fury seizing him, as he tried to make it meet his gaze.

# 14

They came to a river late in the day. At one time there might have been a bridge across it, but now the road ended long before the waterway was even visible. Though quick, the water was barely higher than their knees and they walked across holding their sword and boots above their heads. Once on the other side they rested, filling their canteens, and Vyissan shared the last of his quid with them. A breeze from the north stirred, taking the edge off the sun. It was well at their backs now on its rapid descent, darkness on its heels.

Vyissan was just about to suggest they stay by the river for the evening since there was no better shelter nearby and it would be night soon enough, but Inahan stood and insisted they go. He set a brutal pace, glancing to the northern horizon with nearly every other step.

"What is it?" Vyissan said, his voice sounding more winded than he would have liked.

"We have to get out of here."

He glanced around, unsure what exactly "here" constituted. The desert looked much the same, though the scrub was more plentiful closer to the river and the ground out of the riverbed flatter than normal.

"Look at those."

He was pointing to the northern sky, where Vyissan saw there were clouds gathered. From this distance they looked rather innocuous, neither heavy nor dark and far enough away that he thought it unlikely they would pass anywhere near them. The Enir, he noticed, had not even glanced when Inahan had pointed. *They knew.* He was the only one who apparently had not recognized the signs of the approaching danger, though why they were bothering to outrun a storm was beyond him.

"We have to get to there," Inahan said, pointing to where the flat plain of the river valley abruptly rose to a ridge crowned with a grove of trees. "I don't know how much time we'll have."

Around them the sky remained clear, the afternoon pleasant and warm. A slight breeze stirred. Only the sound of their ragged breathing disturbed the tranquility. Inahan hardly slowed his step when they came to the ridge, which Vyissan saw was much smaller than he had initially thought. They rushed to its peak and then collapsed in the shadows of the trees, eyes closed, waiting for the air to return to them.

Night fell quickly, as it always did in the south, and they set about preparing a fire and a meal. Later, with darkness fully upon them, the wind picked up and the storm arrived, the clouds blotting out the stars and the rain descending in a torrent. It made an overwhelming sound, so much so that he could barely hear the wind and thunder as lightning flashed across the sky. Their fire was soon out and they huddled under some of the brush of the grove, trying vainly to keep dry.

Vyissan happened to be staring into the darkness when a flash of lightning illuminated the landscape they had just crossed, and it was then he saw that it was not only rain making the sound. Below them the river plain had disappeared, replaced by a raging torrent of water. He waited for the next flash to confirm what he could not quite believe and saw again that the river had somehow become a sea, rushing forward unheeded. He shivered and closed his eyes, feeling the rain wash over him, imagining it was that newborn current carrying him to some beyond.

# 15

Cepedutherupt arrived as always, slipping into the city before dawn through one of lesser used gates in a covered palanquin. By all appearances another merchant or noble of rank with business he did not want widely advertised, modestly dressed and with nothing to distinguish him. The palanquin made a circuitous journey through the streets of Lastl before coming to a small estate Keleprai owned, though his family name was not on the record, just for such a purpose. There he disembarked and made his way to the Gver's Palace and the Traitor's Gate where he was admitted by two of Keleprai's most trusted guards and the Master of Offices.

From the Traitor's Gate Nasyren and Cepedutherupt entered the warren of secret passways that ran through the palace, passages that had long provided the Gvers of Lastl with the means to escape attack or to make good on secret assignations and meetings such as this one. They came to a room near in the Gver's quarters of the palace, nearby Keleprai's bedchamber, where a meal had already been set out. Keleprai joined them some minutes later, feigning a headache and excusing himself from his official duties, saying he would take his meal alone in his quarters. He did this often when he intended some delight in the afternoon with a woman and the attendants and courtiers all gave each other sidelong glances and thought no more of the Gver's absence.

He was met by the same unworried face of the High Adept, a hint of a smile forever curling his lips. They exchanged the usual pleasantries and sat down to eat, the Master of Offices absenting himself, no doubt ensuring that two other trusted guards were set at watch outside the door. The High Adept was in a grand mood, especially given the seriousness of the occasion, which took Keleprai aback. He had been dreading this moment from the day he had received the encoded missive, expecting to be told that the Realm was about to fall to ruin, the Great Families about to tear themselves apart. Instead the High Adept wanted only to talk of the impetuousness of their young Qraul.

"He is still a child, of course, but he does not realize it."

"We didn't either at that age. It's a delightful blindness."

"No, I suppose we didn't," Cepedutherupt said, nodding slightly. They sat on either side of a table laden with steaming dishes of food. "He's set on making his mark like his father. He wants to be free of us old men."

"I wish him luck. I thought I would be rid of Tehh as soon as I became Gver, and now I think he'll outlast me."

Keleprai picked at a dish of lentils and duck in a sauce heavy with onions and garlic, wishing they could come to point of the matter so that his stomach might settle enough to enjoy the food on offer. There was an extra plate set at the table for the High Adept's Disciple, who normally attended these meetings, but he was nowhere to be seen. Keleprai did not raise his absence with Cepedutherupt. Adept's kept their own counsel, it was said, and he disliked the man at any rate.

"I hear that we are changing the Sea Challenge," he said, hoping to bring the High Adept around to the point. If there were problems in the Realm, this was where he feared they would lie. A delicate balance had been extablished in the Peninsula and now that it had been disturbed there was no telling what the consequences might be.

The High Adept laughed. "Rakai is in, yes. It's been discussed many times before."

Something must have shown in his face, for Cepedutherupt set his fork down and shrugged his shoulders. "He wants to assert himself, like I said. He wants to take chances and have them pay. There'll be outcry and outrage and all that, but really, the Challenge doesn't mean what it meant in our father's Realm. There's many who will agree."

"Silently," Keleprai said, and Cepedutherupt shrugged again. It was true there was only pride and prestige at stake now with the

Challenge, no trading rights to be gained, but that had, in the strange way of these things, served only to make the competition even more imperative to those involved. He did not believe for an instant that the decision had been Laterala's, either. Cepedutherupt would not stir this hornet's nest without some reason. In truth he agreed with the decision, but the fact that he had not been asked, his agreement assumed, needled at him.

The Adept did not give him a chance to pursue the issue. "Tell me, what news from the border?"

"There was an incursion past the pyrsedies less than a month ago. Nothing unusual and no real consequence. There'll be more activity now that we're coming into summer. There's nothing in the reports to worry."

"My greatest worry is the desert."

Keleprai could not disguise his shock. "In truth? With the Realm as it is?"

"Even so. They will be a grave problem, sooner than you believe. I have given blood to the matter."

Keleprai eyed the Adept. "I suppose this has something to with alkemya and all that. Well, these matters I leave to you of course, but I don't see why we need to worry about the Shadows. We have enough to worry here without going outside the Realm to find it."

"There is no greater threat to the Realm than the spread of the Desecrators false alkemya," the Adept said. "And I have reason to believe this may be happening and it may be spreading into the desert. All I ask, is that you watch those reports."

"Half the Realm debates each morning when they get up whether they will pay fealty to the Qraul or not, and you would like me to pay attention to the wanderings of vagrants."

"Perhaps there is purpose where we see only aimlessness."

Keleprai frowned. "You cannot truly believe that?"

"I don't know, to be honest. Yours is an eye I trust, though."

"I can have the pyrsedies under my command increase their patrols if you would like."

Cepedutherupt nodded his thanks. Keleprai poured himself another measure of wine and resisted a smile. He had no intention of increasing the patrols. Too much expense and bother for what he was certain would come to nothing. There were only the basest of reasons behind what the Shadows did. They wandered the deserts following the seasons in their tribes, striking into Craitol when the opportunity presented itself. They were scavengers—no greater purpose animated or governed them.

Was this truly the reason for this audience, he wondered. To increase the patrols of the desert? A full and complete waste of his day, then. The Adepts were always going on about what they had scried, and more often than not it proved to be of little more worth than what any thaumaturge in any village in the Realm would see in the entrails of an ardeh.

"Have you heard the latest talk from the court?" Cepedutherupt said, turning the conversation again. Keleprai held his hands out. "Well, they are saying that Laterala is a follower of the Lasisen Senteurists."

Keleprai frwoned. "The Apysel? On what basis?"

"His mother," Cepedutherupt said. "She has taken the vows and is living in their cloister."

"What madness has possessed her?"

"Who's to say. But you know as well as I that the boy trusts her word as much as anyone's. Well, everyone knows that. Hence our problem."

Keleprai nodded. The Lasisen Senteurists were a radical sect that worshipped Senteur alone and sought to denigrate the place of Ulternon and Melinon in the theology. According to their belief Senteur was the sole father of humanity, with Melinon little more than an empty receptacle. Many in the Realm favoured Senteur among the Gods, and believed it was he who had triumphed in the struggle among the three, but to exalt him as the sole God of worship was unheard of. There had always been something in Senteurist belief which leaned towards this, but for many, even other Senteurists, it was a step too far.

It was difficult enough, Keleprai knew, for any Gver or Qraul to rule without some suspecting that he favoured this sect or the other. Even choosing among the Morning, Midday, or Evening was fraught with peril, which was why most high nobility followed the choices of their fathers. People were apt to take to the streets if they perceived that some group or other was favoured over their own. He had been careful throughout his rule to play no favourites and be part of the agnostic mass in these things. This was even more dangerous ground, though—if it became accepted that Laterala followed some sect, then no palace would be safe from the mob. The first cloister that Lasisen had built in Lastl had been burned and the Cureders beaten to death.

"When did she do this?" he asked.

"Two months now. I have tried to keep it quiet, but of course it was no use," Cepedutherupt said. "You know her better than I—you grew up together, did you not? Send word to her, try to speak reason."

A rap at the door interrupted them. They both turned, frowning, to stare at its blank visage before Keleprai got to his feet and went to open it, a few choice words for Nasyren already on his lips. Before he reached the door it swung open and someone he didn't recognize stepped through. A short, compact man, his dark shade suggesting he was from the Mgetir Isle, wearing the dress of a palace attendant. He had his mouth open to yell at the Master of Offices for allowing this unforgivable breach of protocol—the High Adept was here in secret, for Gods' sake, you couldn't allow some attendant to just come wandering in—when he saw the man had a dagger in hand.

He fumbled for the ceremonial dagger he always had at his side, but the attacker was already upon him, thrusting the dagger at his throat. Keleprai managed to stave off the blow, grasping the man's wrist and holding him at bay. While they struggled, Keleprai called out to the guards who should have been at the outer doors of the quarters. There was no response and the attacker gave him a grim smile.

"Hold," Cepedutherupt said in a voice gone cavernous, freezing the intruder momentarily. It was enough that Keleprai was able to extract himself and get his own dagger free. The attacker eyed the two of them warily, holding his dagger out before him.

Glancing over, Keleprai saw the High Adept's eyes begin to change, glazing in the way that all Adepts and their Disciples did when practicing their art, as if they had become unhinged from the rest of their body. It would be over quickly now, he thought. Once Cepedutherupt had the attacker under control he could step in and finish him.

Just as he thought they had victory easily within their grasp, he saw the assassin's eyes turn as well. He did not have time to brace himself before the alkemy hit him like a sharp gust of wind. The very floor he stood on was unstable; it was something like being on the sea in a storm. There was the same trembling, the plunging of his stomach to his bowels and the sudden chance that his insides might come rushing out of his body.

The assassin and Cepedutherupt were locked in a desperate struggle, unseen but for the grim tautness of their faces. Keleprai tried to take a step forward, to intercede in some way, but he doubled over, clutching his head in agony as the alkemy flooded the air. It was too near him, all this power, and he was only feeling the excess spilling over from the battle. His body felt numb and his nose started to run so that he wondered if it was bleeding.

When he at last managed to raise his head he found himself looking upon an almost absurd scene. The assassin was moving towards the High Adept with painstaking slowness, as though he were terrified the ground beneath was about to fall away. At the same time Cepedutherupt was immobile, seemingly not aware of the other at all. Desperately, Keleprai tried to intervene, but he fell to his knees with his first step. The alkemy crackled in his ears, but he knew there was no sound being formed, just as there was nothing visible in the air. It was all in the realm of the spirits.

By the time Keleprai regained his feet the assassin had buried his knife to the hilt in Cepedutherupt's side. He yanked it free with a triumphant gasp. The High Adept's expression remained unchanged, and as quickly as it had come the intruder's grin vanished. His hand remained in the air, holding the dagger at an odd angle while he screamed as he was suffused in a white glare. Smoke started to rise off him and his eyes rolled back into his head, his tongue flopping out of his mouth. Finally, he collapsed to the ground in a heap.

The stench of burnt flesh was overwhelming. Keleprai was left reeling. His body felt raw and stiff, like he had been lashed and beaten for hours. Cepedutherupt, he saw, had fallen to the ground. The silence was oppressive and he wondered if he had somehow lost his hearing during the battle.

He forced himself to his feet, fighting the vertigo, which was still overwhelming in the aftermath of the alkemy. He managed only a step before he went to his knees and retched, sending the meal he had just eaten to the floor. That made him feel better, though, and he got back to his feet and walked over to the assassin, pushing him onto his back with his foot. Having assured himself of the man's demise, Keleprai stumbled out of the room and down the hallway to find Nasyren.

# 16

Masiph id Ezern was born the fourth of four sons, a foul omen it was said—and it quickly proved to be so, for his mother died mere hours after his birth. The attending healer, sensing the delicate nature of his situation, laid the blame upon the newborn for being too large for the birth canal. That the child was a fourth son was left unsaid, though it was on the mind of everyone within hearing. In the end it mattered not what the healer said—he was executed for his failure to save the life of the wife of one of the most important Nohritai in Darrhyn. Ibrazol mourned his wife, keeping vigil over her tomb the standard ten days. The healer was hanged in Execution Square in front of small group of jeering spectators and his body, naked from the waist up and carved with symbols marking him a traitor to the throne, was displayed atop the city wall near the Anar Gate for two weeks.

When he took to feeling sorry for himself, Masiph would wonder about what life might have been like had his mother survived his birth. He had been told more times than he could count that his parents had been a true match, though it was difficult for him to conceive his father professing love to anyone. Many said, sympathy touching their voices, that things would surely have been different for him had his mother survived. Ibrazol was never the same after, they murmured—how could he be?

Those were nothing more than platitudes, though. One could see the lie of it just by comparing Ibrazol to his first three sons, for they were all of a piece. It was Masiph who did not match the rest.

He had none of their quiet competency, nothing of their reserve. That, more than anything, explained the fraught relationship between father and son. Nothing that marked the Ezern could be seen in him, not in the way that it had his brothers. Or his cousin, Khibar id Ezern, the second to the Vazeir of Enwaless Province, if it came to that. And when it came time to decide who would stand for the Ad Ezern, Masiph knew it would.

All this was to say that it did not surprise him in the least that his father had yet to intercede on his behalf in the three weeks since his audience with the Ad Eselte and his coronation into the army. Three weeks and he had not been elevated to the ranks, had been given no word of what unit he would be leading. When he had pressed for any information he was told that Vazeir Gheyuth id Lelletl had granted him some leave as a reward for his efforts and to ensure his full recovery. There was no way this was some kind of accident; he had not been misplaced in any bureaucratic shuffling. Someone, his father—Gheyuth, the Emperor, who was to say—did not want him elevated in the ranks.

It had been two years since he had come of age and his father had never once discussed a marriage for him either, though he was the only son remaining to Ibrazol. Yet it seemed clear, at least in deed if not in thought, that Ibrazol saw his nephew as the better man to lead the family after his passing. He had arranged for his position as second to the Vazeir as well as his marriage into the Ad Beiron, an important southern family. Masiph had neither of these, though he was only a year younger than his cousin. And until he did he had no standing within the family or without.

So he waited, keeping quiet, pretending that this was normal procedure and that it was simply a matter of time before he assumed his new post. Every chance public encounter became an exercise in humiliation as a result, for there was always the praise and hearty congratulations on his coronation followed by the inevitable question about when he was to be elevated. And he had to smile and shrug and prevaricate. It always left him infuriated and disgusted with himself that he did not do something about this outrage. Spit in the face of those who insulted him and go to Vazeir Gheyuth and demand his elevation.

Instead he had spent three weeks in utter aimlessness, wandering the districts till his boot soles were thin. He had been to each of the nine markets, once almost buying a parrot before reason contained him, and any number of drinkeries where he knew he could find some other young Husems who would be more than willing to share cups with him. Anywhere but his own quarters, which he hated. He despised the whole estate, and, since his wet nurse had died of the fevers, he hadn't trusted any of the servants or eunuchs. They were his father's people, assigned to watch him and report on his activities. It all left him feeling ensnared in a labyrinth of nothing, not even a whisper of air passing through the obscured pathways.

Today, though, he had determined would be different. He would not spend it moping about until a dull lethargy took hold and he spent the afternoon in bed. Because there seemed nothing else for it, he would spend the day in drinking and whatever followed it. He started with a mug of dalan sweetened with a liqueur of nuts and peaches when he rose late in the morning, and then wandered from the Ad Ezern estate to a tavern on the edge of the district. He planned to spend the day in various drinkeries, beginning in the more fashionable places where he was likely to run across someone he knew who would be willing to spend the day in cups with him, and from there moving on to establishments of lesser repute.

When it came to noon and he had gone through the better part of four cups of bitters, and no one he knew had made an appearance, he decided to push on to an inn just down the street which he knew served a fine meal. He was joined there by Hatan id Duerienn, a slight acquaintance from one of the lesser Nohritai families. Hatan had some asyl flower, and once they finished their sustenance they retreated to the alley of the inn to share a vial of the nectar. It went down well, but Masiph's head was soon throbbing and his whole body felt swollen—especially his stomach, which was ballooning from the beer, the meal and the nectar. The street beyond the alley looked like a finely painted glass that had been shattered and then pieced back together haphazardly.

Hatan had other engagements for the afternoon, so Masiph decided to strike out from the inn on his own. He left the Uenam, deciding it would be best to be away from the district in his coming state where he would be unlikely to run into any of the greater Nohritai. Best to avoid giving his father or Gheyuth any further reason to withhold his elevation.

Two days before, Osiphan id Reteln had surprised him in a

drinkery along with a couple of acquaintances of lesser quality, only one a Nohritai, and he a known derelict. Husem Osiphan had asked to speak with him and Masiph, stammering, went along, cursing for allowing himself to be caught in such a situation. All he could think as he followed the Husem to a table in the dark of the room, out of sight of the door, was that if his father heard of any of this he would not be elevated, to say nothing of talk of marriage, for a decade.

They had begun with the standard pleasantries, and then a not entirely idle inquiry after Masiph's health. When he answered that he had been well for the last several weeks, Husem Osiphan nodded, his expression a picture of concern.

"It is unfortunate that your elevation has yet to be granted."

Masiph agreed with him, as it seemed prudent. "Still," he said, "they have given me leave out of respect for my service Husem and my sacrifice on the night of the raid."

"But it has been three weeks. Are they women following the ebbing of the moon?"

Masiph shrugged. They were venturing toward dangerous territory.

"The appearance of it, you see, suggests less than honorable motives on the part of someone," the Nohritai said. "Perhaps I could discuss this with Husem Gheyuth and see if I can see what the delay is."

"No," Masiph said. "No, that is quite all right. Thank you, Husem. But it is not necessary."

The best way to ensure he would never live to see his elevation was if the head of the Ad Reteln spoke on his behalf. There had been rumors when the previous Ad Eselte had died, a strange affair to say the least, that placed young Osiphan and a few other notables at the center of a conspiracy. He had backed a cousin when the current Emperor had succeeded his father to the Imperial throne, supported by the Ad Ezern. These things were not forgotten, not easily, and not without a great deal of time.

"It is simply," Husem Osiphan said, with an apologetic smile, "that it is incredible to me that someone as young and spiritful as yourself, someone of sound mind and of good family, is left to rot on the vine, unmarried and unelevated, when so fruitful."

"Well, as I say, Husem, I have every confidence that it will work out."

"Perhaps you are right. Patience is the wisest course, as the sages say. I just can't help but feel disappointed with the foolishness of our Most Gracious Emperor and his advisers, who either do not realize or do not see fit to use the talents of the Nohritai who desire only greatness for the empire."

Masiph sat rigidly, unable to even meet the Husem's eyes. It felt like he had been stricken by some virulent form of paralysis. His mind fumbled with words, but no response came forth. He looked around, hoping to catch a server's eye so that he might have his cup filled again.

"I'm sorry for speaking so," Osiphan said. "But it is shortsighted, and that is a failing of this regime, and has been for some time. How can we expect to return to our former glories if we do not strive to do so? I am only too familiar with it. It infects everything."

Osiphan stood up, signaling that their conversation was at a close, and Masiph joined him, even as his body sagged with relief. They each gave their farewells and then Osiphan raised his hand as though he had just recalled something.

"I understand you would rather I not intercede on your behalf. Likely that is the best course. But I would encourage you to join me and some others, young men like yourself, where we have the chance to give voice to such concerns as I have to you. It is a private meeting, of course. If you sit at this table three nights from today, an hour past sundown, someone will meet you and bring you to the place."

"Thank you for concern, Husem. Thank you for the invitation."

Osiphan had waved his hand, as if to say what was this small thing between such friends as they? "There is spirit in your blood. Some of us have not forgotten Walleen. I see it in you. Used wisely it can lead to great things."

And that, of everything in their conversation, he decided had been the most baffling. The spirit of Walleen. Even he, who admired the man's conviction, had to admit the utter folly of his enterprise. His own followers had murdered him somewhere in the desert when they had realized there was no grand victory against the Shadows, as they melted into the landscape at the sight of the Renian force. Disease had struck as they sought to return to the Empire and the Shadow Men had harassed them all the way to the border. Of the five hundred who set out, only one hundred returned, starved and nearly as mad as Walleen himself.

No, it was ludicrous that Osiphan id Reteln of all people would praise the man, although no less ludicrous than his apparent invitation for Masiph to join him in some sort of conspiracy against the Ad Eselte. Even hinting at such actions terrified him. Still, he could not help but be intrigued all the same, at the opportunity, no matter how false and illusory, to join a quest to right the wrongs of this realm. But this was the worst sort of petty intrigue and nothing more. The only reason Osiphan would want to involve him was because he saw an opportunity to embarrass the Ad Ezern and maybe even the Emperor. And yet, the thought of Ibrazol in a fury beyond reason was not an unhappy one.

The asyl nectar continued to blossom within him, and his confused senses led him on some vaguely remembered route in Edelin District west of the Aesencanal. The narrow streets were dirt in all but a few places, and there the stone was broken. All the buildings seemed to be shambling contraptions, leaning here and there, their purpose unclear. He went into the first drinkery he passed, a ruinous place that he imagined groaned under a strong wind. It smelled of rotten alcohol and spoiled meat, among other less distinguishable scents. A long table with two benches provided the only seats, the other side of the room taken up by a bar counter, and behind that a fireplace and casks of beer.

There were two men at the table, their heads close together as they spoke. Both glanced up when he entered, the light from outside momentarily casting away the gloom within. They stared at him for a moment then turned back to their conversation. He sat near the door and studied them. They were clearly criminals of some sort, he decided, wondering what they might be plotting.

A girl, wraithlike in the shadows, came up to him and he asked for a cup of ale. There was a hardness about her face that made it difficult to say just how old she might be, and a deadness to her eyes that left him uneasy. She brought him a slopping mug of something and he watched her go. He wondered how much it might cost to take her upstairs. Going at her with the heat and this stench and gloom might take the edge of the asyl, which had him sweating and jittery.

He sipped at what she had brought him and was glad it was too dark for him to get a clear look. He worried for a second that he fallen to the floor, but no, there he was, his hand still on his mug.

He glanced over at his two miscreant companions, but they had disappeared. When had that happened, he wondered, and how long had he been here?

He noticed the girl watching him from behind the counter. She came over and brought him another mug. He watched her as she moved around behind the counter, her face unchanging, her only stray movement an unconscious gesture to brush her hair back though it wasn't near her eyes. The two men had returned, or perhaps he had been mistaken and they had never left. One of them caught him looking at them, and he quickly busied himself studying the casks.

It seemed a good idea to stay here and wait out the rains before he moved on. They could not be far off now. The girl, it appeared, had brought him another cup of the awful stuff. Had he already finished the other?

"I am telling you, he is a demon," he overheard one of the men say. "When did he join us?"

"Not long after the attack."

"Exactly. You really think they caught them all? I mean, with the Watch you might as well just leave the gates open."

The other said something Masiph couldn't hear, and then his companion replied, "We have to kill him, I think. He'll be at our throats as soon as he's the chance."

Though he knew they were not talking about him, he still felt nervous. The asyl nectar did not help. The shadows seemed to loom on his periphery, heavy and jagged, working at his building paranoia. Perhaps he would see about the girl after all. Better to be upstairs with her than overhearing some murderous plot.

He called her over and asked for her price, but she seemed not to comprehend. He repeated himself, the sharpness of his voice drawing stares from the other two men and surprising even himself. More concerning was that the words sounding in his mind were not leaving his tongue in any identifiable form. The girl shrugged and brought him another cup. He grabbed her wrist as she turned to go, and then she understood what he was about. She led him, not upstairs, but out into the alley behind the tavern, and there amidst the effluvia and refuse she knelt to service him.

# 17

It was the stench of alkemy and burnt flesh that told Disciple Hieran why he and Adept Tehh had been summoned into the presence of the Gver by the Master of Offices. As they came to the chambers, the guard parting to let them through, they saw the High Adept of the Council being carried out on a stretcher, bleeding from a wound in his chest and unconscious. Hieran heard his own breath being drawn in sharply. Tehh turned to him with a stern look on his face, as if to say: *Now is not the time to embarrass me with your melodramatics.*

They passed through the outer chamber to the inner and found Gver Keleprai sitting on a chair, ashen faced, looking down at a burnt corpse.

"What happened here, Most Immortal?" Tehh said.

"Alkemya. He had alkemya and..." Keleprai managed, ending with a gesture at the corpse. Tehh nodded and turned to eye the body, and then glanced at Hieran.

Without needing to be told, he bowed to the Gver and left the room, going to the hall where the two guards stood. They were all experienced soldiers, none of them showing the anxiety they must be feeling having allowed an assassin into the chambers of the Gver. Their lives were now very much in the hands of others—his, for starters.

"You were here the entire time?"

"Yes, Disciple," one of them replied, presumably the senior among them.

"And you heard nothing? Saw nothing?"

"The first we knew something was cracked was from the smell. We tried the door," he said, "but it was charmed."

Hieran did not bother to tell the man that the Council Adepts and their enemies did not traffic in charms, those were province of witches and thaumaturges, all those ignorant of true alkemya. In fact, he said nothing more to any of them, leaving their worry to fester, and returned to the outer chamber. A sniff of the door confirmed that it had been barred by the attacker, and a quick search of the room itself revealed nothing. He stood at its center for a moment, clicking his tongue against the roof of his mouth. His first guess—the fireplace—was wrong, but the second—an arras of Melinon being taken by Senteur and Ulternon—concealed the chamber's secret doorway. Leave it to the Alastl to think with their badges, he thought, as he fumbled with the door's mechanism.

After some anguished moments where he feared he might have to retreat to the inner chamber and ask the Gver or, Gods forbid, Tehh for assistance—all the more embarrassing since the man still smoldering on the floor had managed the trick of it—the door sprang free, swinging back to expose the shadowed passageway behind. He nodded to himself, clicking his tongue again, and stepped into the passage, being careful to keep a hand at the door so it didn't swing closed behind him.

He needn't have worried; the assassin had left his lantern lit, no doubt expecting to need a quick escape. Beside the lantern and within its glow he saw what Tehh had sent him to find. It was one of the smallest that he had seen, an intricate mass of intestinal glass tubing wrapping around and around on itself. At its base was a pan, dark with resin, the stench of its burnt remains still clinging to the apparatus, which was used to heat the quicksilver and set it spinning. He could see the bright turquoise element pooling at rest near the bowl and shivered, feeling, even now, the astral it cast off in its latent state.

He strode forward, letting the door swing shut behind him, and seized the engine only to let it go with a cry and curse. Though the quicksilver was latent and the pan had burnt itself out, the tubes were still scalding to the touch. The pain echoed outward from his hand into an ever-widening sphere, giving him the sensation of having a giant appendage hanging off his arm. It was only as the throbbing of his hand dulled that he realized all his flailing about had somehow put the lantern out. His curses reverberated down the dark and empty hallway.

# 18

They entered the Renuih Empire late the next day. There was a tower beside the road, but otherwise nothing that would indicate they were now in a civilized land. The desert stretched on to the edge of the horizon, the same awe-inspiring distance as always, and there was no sign of habitation anywhere, excepting the tower. There were two men visible on watch as they walked past, who gave them a cursory glance before returning their eyes to the road. Four mud-stained men from parts unknown wandering in from the wild desert was apparently unworthy of further note.

Vyissan was struck by the unchanging landscape as he passed from one realm to another, though in all likelihood the border with Craitol was much the same. The Gods recognized none of the vanity of empire, as any student of history could well judge. All their arbitrary lines, drawn by swords in the earth, the wind soon to blow them awry.

They arrived at Sylaron just before midday the next day, the desert having gradually dissipated, the hardy and gnarled scrub replaced by more supple and delicate greens. The highway wound through several villages, scratching out what looked to Vyissan like a meager existence so precariously exposed near the desert and its insidious threat. And then they came to the river and at its center was the city itself, teeming to overflowing on an island. The Resnan was so large it hardly seemed to be a river, its opposite bank just visible beyond the city in the still hazy air. He had long heard stories of the river's magnitude, but seeing it firsthand defied even those descriptions. Seagoing vessels were docked at the Sylaron ports and the coast was not anywhere in sight.

They crossed over to the city on the public ferries, and Inahan guided them all to the lending house where Vyissan had his letter of introduction. He had them wait outside in the event that he encountered any difficulties, for he was unsure of himself around the beardless Renians, but it was all as he had been told. He paid the swords in full and thanked them, clasping each of their arms, and they went on their separate paths, the two Enir south to the docks to see what work lay there and Inahan to the west and whatever awaited him.

Vyissan headed north to the heart of the city. He would need to find a boat for the journey north, but if it was as he had been told that would be an easy matter. Ships passed up and down the river at all times, which had been evident as they came down through the river valley. It could well wait for tomorrow, he decided. For today, a chew and a woman.

He found the aslyn without incident and had the end of a quid in his lip as he followed the directions of the man who had sold it to him down the unfamiliar streets. He had just spotted the oddly colored rooster above the door to some drinkery which the man had told him about when a familiar sensation crept through his mind. It was a distant, vague feeling, and the itching that, as always, made him want to reach out, to touch what was not there was only more pronounced as a result.

It enveloped him lightly and then, just as it had come, it dissipated to nothing. This was so unexpected that he called out in his own tongue, a loud report that carried down the street above the general hubbub of the city. He stopped in midstride, nearly falling as he did so, and whispered to himself "Gods preserve me," feeling his lips move as he did so. In that instant, as he cursed himself as the greatest of idiots to ever walk this realm, he could see this unfolding disaster proceeding to his doom. The Imperial Magistery seizing him, the search of his pouch and the discovery of what lay within, the peering through his disguise to the shade below.

Every moment could count now, as they so rarely did. People walked around him, giving him a wide berth as they made warding signs. There were no Imperial agents that he could see, and those who had heard his outburst seemed to be treating him as little more than one touched by a daemon. *They had no daemons here. Only ancestors.* He could hear his pulse, thunderous, in his temple. The air seemed ready to smother him. He had to go, he realized, get off this street and away from this crowd before he betrayed himself absolutely.

The episode, the hardships of his journey across the desert, and Nesyur's face, which was always there now when he closed his eyes, all reached a terrible confluence within him and he ran, shoving people out of his way as he did so, for the nearest alley he could find. There he was sick, retching on the ground while his bowels spilled forth of their own accord soiling his robes. He slumped against the nearest wall, not even caring about the filth around him, his fear dissolving into exhaustion.

# 19

Hieran shifted uncomfortably under the gaze of the High Adept, wondering again why Tehh had requested that he accompany him to this encounter, when the Lastl Adept never included him in meetings with the Gver or anyone of importance, unless the Council was gathering and he needed someone to pass notes.

"Your concern is appreciated, but not warranted," Cepedutherupt said, at last taking his eyes from Hieran. "I am quite well."

"Why have you graced us with your presence here in Lastl, if I may be so bold? I did not know you were traveling this way."

"I came to speak with the Immortal Gver. I was to be in the vicinity anyway and thought it would be opportune to discuss some matters of the Realm," Cepedutherupt said, a smile forced about his lips.

Hieran had to resist a smile himself—they might as well be spitting at one another, for the venom was thick beneath their tongues.

The High Adept tried to raise himself up from his pillow so that he was sitting to face them, but his countenance was immediately marred by pain. Tehh took a step forward as though to assist him, only to be met by Cepedutherupt's furious glare and Hieran thanked the Gods in all their infinite glory that he had been allowed to witness this. He had to admire, grudgingly, the way Tehh was proceeding—the doddering old man could hardly lift a pillow, let alone the High Adept—his solicitous concern so corrosive Hieran was worried it might dissolve the floor beneath them.

"You remember what we spoke about at the Council last spring? It did not seem worth the trouble of an official visit."

"Hardly," Tehh said as Hieran struggled to recall what, in fact, the Council had discussed in the spring.

"Though it has become more troublesome than I anticipated."

"Most certainly."

"I should ask you, since you would know the signs as well as I. What do you think the Shadows are about?"

"The demons are as constant as the seasons. They do not change. It is not in their nature."

Hieran remembered now, the High Adept had been obsessed with the Shadows and their doings. This in spite of the fact that the insurrection against the Council and Craitol still flourished in the dark and squalid corners of the Realm, those places most fertile for the vanquished. It had been odd then, though the High Adept had always seemed peculiar to the Disciple, and it was bizarre now given what had just occurred in the Gver's chambers.

The High Adept was unable to stifle a sigh. "You know as well as I that is not the case."

"Do I?" Tehh walked slowly around the bed to the window at the far end of the chamber. "I know what your claims were this spring. As you know, I was not convinced then. I remain unconvinced. You credit them too much. They cannot manage to construct a village, yet you would grant them the Realm."

"Can you not read the signs when they are written plain for all to see?"

Had he said much the same thing twelve years ago when Kercubegahedd had begun his insurrection in the northern wilds of Kragi? No, Hieran thought, then the Council had been blind to the danger he presented. They had been safe in their view of a realm ordered by the Gods' hands that placed them at the exalted center and they had paid no mind to the northerner of little distinction who saw fit to spurn them after he was judged a Disciple. That a Disciple, with his band of followers, who possessed even less faculty than he, could nearly manage to destroy the Council perhaps explained the High Adept's vigilance now with regards to the Shadows. If a northerner were capable of such feats, perhaps they were as well.

Tehh, of course, put little value in the High Adept's coin.

"Perhaps they are in a language I am not versed in. Few of the Council seem able to translate them as you do, if I remember rightly."

"I know what I have seen. It will come to pass if we do not act."

"If you look for threats, often you will find them."

"Do we know the assassin?" Cepedutherupt said, clearly deciding to continue this battle another day, one where he might hope to have the upper hand. Or at least one where he had not just been gutted by some no-rank assassin while in the midst of a clandestine meeting in another Adept's realm.

The Adept of Lastl shook his head and gestured to his Disciple. "We found this," he said as Hieran drew the now cooled engine out from within his robes. He resisted wincing as he did so, the embarrassment of locking himself in the darkened passageway stinging more than his hand.

"Where?"

"In the passway."

"Who knows of them?" Cepedutherupt asked.

"I do," Tehh said, gesturing to Hieran as he did so. "The Master of Offices as well. The wife of the Gver, and Keleprai himself."

He paused after saying it, as though there were another name to add, but he said no more. There was no need, for all three of them recognized that the High Adept knew the passways as well. How else, after all, had he passed through the palace undetected? As had the assassin. They must nearly have trodden upon each other, Hieran thought, and saw by his expression that Cepedutherupt was thinking the same thing.

That such a man, of no rank or quality, could nearly end the life of the High Adept of the Council was almost unfathomable to Hieran. It had been unfathomable until ten years ago, but now they lived in a realm fallen, or reborn, depending upon your persuasion.

"There will be an investigation, obviously," the High Adept said.

"Yes. The Gver has asked me to see to it."

Cepedutherupt said nothing, his face expressionless.

"One wonders at your fascination with the Shadows when we are visited with such depredations by those within our borders."

"My concern with the Shadows is not an exclusive one. It grows from my concern with those of Kercubegahedd's followers who still remain. They will ally with anyone, both within the Realm and without. We have to stay vigilant or their evil will spread like a weed, and you and I know the consequence of that."

"Yes, we do." Tehh turned away from the bed. "I should go, though," he said. "You'll be wanting to rest."

He made his way towards the door, Hieran in tow, and then halted abruptly, as if something had only just occurred to him. He turned to the High Adept. "Should I let someone know to have a room prepared for your Disciple? I don't imagine you were planning on spending the evening, but you will have to now."

And now Hieran knew why he had been asked to attend with the Adept of Lastl, his presence a signal to the High Adept that Tehh knew his Disciple had not accompanied him. How could he know, Hieran wondered.

"No need," Cepedutherupt said. "I left my Disciple in Craitol so that the court might think I was still about. Seemed wise in the moment."

"Clever, no doubt," Tehh said, and they left the room.

As they walked back to the Adept's quarters, Hieran a step behind his master, he thought, as he often did, about Kercubegahedd's rejection of his discipledom. He had often wished that he had possessed the wisdom to do so himself when the judgement of the Council had been given him. To not suffer under the hands of such a man as Tehh, the thought always left him delirious. An old fool lost to his trivial studies and ancient quarrels. How different his life might have been. Still, standing against the Council was a sure way to shorten one's time in this realm, as today's events made evident, and in the end he was no hero. He would not risk himself for a cause, no matter its justice. He was just a man, as small and petty as the one who ruled his days.

# 20

The streets were slick with rain, the sun hidden behind the clouds. The heat was oppressive still, the air vaporous with the humidity and the leftover rain. Masiph had the urge to start swimming through the veil of atmosphere that had been draped over them. The narrow streets seemed to be spiraling around in ever-shrinking circles, as though they were guiding him to some fated destination. He struggled against it for a time, even doubling back on his path, all to no effect until he relented and went as the road would take him.

He stood on the edge of the field watching several units at practice with lance formations while others wrestled or fought hand to hand with blunted daggers. Soldiers saluted as they passed him, clasping their left shoulder with their right hand, and officers nodded their respect. Husem Gheyuth id Lelletl, Vazeir of the Army, strode by with his coterie on his way to his offices. Catching a glimpse of Masiph from the corner of his eye, he stopped and then walked towards him, motioning for the others to stay behind. Masiph saluted the Vazeir, who looked at him with a puzzled and apologetic expression.

Someone swore at them, startling them both. "Mind your path, fool."

Masiph found himself facing a pair of swords, two menacing Atenan mercenaries grasping them. A haughty-looking merchant stood behind them, dressed pompously in violet Craitolian silk robes and a hat of what appeared to be leopard fur, in spite of the heat. He stared at them all curiously and looked about to see where he was. Sensing the start of a crowd forming to watch what might turn into an afternoon spectacle, he simply nodded at the men and walked on.

It once would have been a wonder to see a merchant walking the streets of a respectable neighborhood with an armed guard, no matter the degree of his wealth. Since the raid it had become a common enough sight. Masiph had emerged after his recovery to a city that gave the appearance of being under siege, though there had been no attacks since, nor had there been any shadows spotted in the vicinity of the capital as far as he knew. One never saw the enclosed palanquin of a Nohritai lady without an armed escort anymore, and more and more of the Nohritai and the wealthy took one as well. Never mind that a conniving brother or a drunken scofflaw was more likely to visit ill upon them than one of the Shadows.

His mind was still dull and fogged from the nectar, his throat dry from the heat and too much beer and walking. Though his focus still came and went, he made his way toward the barracks, a circuitous route, his momentary vision inspiring him to action. It was well into the afternoon before he passed the three inner walls and reached his destination. A guard stood at the gate, looking attentively bored. Masiph approached, expecting him to step aside and allow him entry, but the guard stood his ground.

"Husem, your name please?" he asked in a dull voice.

Masiph stared at him. "Does this," he said, gesturing at the blue of his robe, "not allow me entrance? I have a cousin I wish to see."

The guard sighed. "New procedures, Husem. We are not to let anyone in, even a Nohritai, without their having been put on our day list."

"And why is that?"

The guard sighed more loudly. "No one is to be allowed into the barracks unless they are sulihers or they are to meet a suliher and that suliher has cleared it with his jetthir and his jetthir has put that person's name on the day list. Your name, Husem?"

"Masiph id Ezern," he said in his most authoritative voice.

"You are not on the list, Husem," the guard said without a glance down.

"How do you know? You haven't even looked at it."

"Everyone who was on the list has already come and left. It is getting late in the day after all, Husem," he said.

"If you already knew, why bother asking, suliher?"

"New procedures, Husem," the guard said.

"I was unaware of the new procedures, obviously, and my cousin failed to mention them. But I do need to see him. You cannot possibly believe that someone of the Ad Ezern would be a threat to the empire."

The guard shrugged. "I really couldn't say, Husem, but I cannot let you in. New procedures. I could try sending one of the runners to find him, but if his cohort is at their exercises he won't be able to come. Best, Husem, if you leave a message with me and your cousin can organize another day."

Masiph shook his head and looked around to see if anyone on the street was watching, but there were only a couple of shop assistants on their way home. He squinted at the guard, struggling for the moment to focus on him. "If I didn't need to see him today I would simply let him get a leave and meet him in the city."

"I understand, Husem, but the new procedures..." the guard began.

"I would like to speak with your jetthir," Masiph said.

The guard shrugged and called over his shoulder, and another suliher came from the guardhouse beside the gate.

"Husem would like to see the Jetthir," the guard said. The second suliher raised his eyebrow and the guard simply shrugged. The soldier called for Masiph to follow him and opened the gate. They left the guard to close it and went into the small building immediately adjacent to the entrance. Inside there were three men dicing around a makeshift table. They walked past them and into the next room, where the jetthir sat writing at a table. He rose as they entered and the suliher saluted.

Masiph waited until the soldier was dismissed before speaking, explaining that he needed to speak with his cousin.

"Masiph den Ibrazol," the jetthir said in the tone of a judge pronouncing his sentence. "Is that why you are here?"

"Yes," Masiph said, uncertainty striking him like a closed fist. He did not recognize the jetthir, though the man clearly knew him, whether personally or by name. He found himself staring at the inkpot on the jetthir's desk, unable to find any words to say, a chill gripping him.

"I'm sorry, Jetthir," he said finally, "I did not get your name."

"Ollen id Dynnes," the jetthir replied. A lesser family. His accent suggested he was from Ferrynn, so Masiph doubted they would have ever crossed paths.

"I had expected you would have joined us by now," the jetthir added. "We heard of your coronation, what was it, three weeks ago? You seem to have recovered of your wounds, ancestors grant that it is so. Perhaps not though. They say some wounds can scald the mind."

Masiph cleared his throat, trying to fight the gnawing sense that the situation was going horribly wrong. He exhaled, more loudly than he had intended. "It is not for me to determine, Jetthir. It is for the Husem Gheyuth."

"Of course. Naturally," the jetthir said in a sneering tone. "What cousin, pray tell Husem, are you looking for? There are no Ad Ezern that I know in the army. Certainly none posted here."

"He is from my mother's family. Jetthir Husem Geullar id Adragem of the seventh quadra."

"Ah yes. The seventh quadra has been stationed in Eles for some months now."

His eyes finally found the jetthir's. There was a look of complete disdain on his face and Masiph immediately realized with a brutal clarity how he must look, disheveled and drunken, reeking of sex and concoction, his clothes a storm-bedraggled mess.

"I, I must have misunderstood his message, perhaps."

"Of course," the jetthir replied. Masiph took his leave, unable to meet the jetthir's eyes again, and fled the room and building. He went headlong without a glance at the suliher and then was forced to stop as the soldier followed behind him and let him out. He walked away as fast as he could, fighting the urge to turn back and see if they were watching him go.

That, he realized, had been his first time inside the barrack walls since he and his father had gone to claim the body of his brother, Adizen, who had perished from desert fever five years ago, making it three sons lost in service to the Empire. The first two had died in battle against Shadow Men raiders. Ibresuul's, the eldest, was a hero's death, standing alone against a demon horde to allow his fellow suliheri, the remnants of his cohort, time to escape to their boats and set into the Resnasn before he fell to the sword. Songs had been written and Masiph knew it had been mentioned in several chronicles as well. He had been little more than five then, the youngest in the family by ten years. Though they all inhabited the same estate, they hardly crossed paths in their years together, especially once the rest joined the army when they reached age.

It came to him as he slowed his pace and began to assess his situation that the barracks were near Nustef's home. Heading there was a more palatable option for the moment than attempting to cross the city again, especially as nightfall was near. He couldn't hope to make it to Uenam before dark, even if he could find a palanquin for hire in this district.

There was some difficulty finding the street—the district was set in the hills that rolled out of the river valley and the roads were set at all angles as the topography demanded. He knew that he was looking for a particular staircase that slanted up a hill, connecting to a street above, but he had difficulty picking out which stairs led to streets. It did not help that all the buildings looked similar in the growing darkness, simple and rundown for the most part, a chronicle on various states of dereliction. The fevers had struck the district in the dry season and many of the buildings were still marked with the sign of the contagion.

He found it at last, a staircase that did lead somewhere, and he began to count the buildings he passed. When he came to seven he ducked through the gate to the courtyard and found the stairs that led to the upper level. A hush settled around him as he went by open doors and caught glimpses of the apartments within. Eyes from expressionless faces stared back at him, surrounded by the glare of light. He came to a door and then glanced down to the courtyard below to orient himself before knocking.

After a long wait the door opened a crack and a face obscured by shadow peered out at him. He attempted an inviting smile, introducing himself and asking for Nustef. The door widened a bit and light from a lamp cast out some of the gloom so that he could see that it was a woman.

"Nustef is not in, Husem," she said in a low voice. "He is on the wall for patrol."

"Oh," he said, taken aback. "Of course."

He stared stupidly at her, trying to remember her name. Nustef had spoken of her often, but this was the first time he had seen her. She was extraordinary really, he thought, although her face was quite plain. Something in the eyes. The light moved in them like a tide rising higher. Perhaps it was the aftereffects of the nectar.

*Erise*, it came then. His mother's name, actually. A popular name among the Nohritai in his mother's youth, though one did not hear it often now.

"I hadn't thought of it, lady Erise," he said quickly as she apologized. "Of course he would be. I was just, you see, over at the barracks visiting my cousin. He is a jetthir in the seventh cohort. On my mother's side, a cousin. So I don't get to see him as much as I would like, you know. Although he is posted in the capital. So I was done talking with him and I thought that I had time to stop in and see Nustef. But I hadn't thought that he wouldn't be here."

She smiled nervously and nodded, looking behind him into the settling evening. Noticing that he realized how this must look: a Nohritai calling on a woman of no standing, married at that, after dark. The silence of the courtyard and apartments around him seemed different then, not an absence but a presence, dozens of ears leaning forward to catch what this loud, drunken fool was saying and watching to see what Erise would do in response. The exhaustion that he had been holding at bay started to seep through his body, the drink and nectar no longer enough to sustain him.

He apologized for disturbing her so late in the day and she smiled again, this time gratefully. He watched her shut the door, leaving him in the shadows of the dusk broken by the lamplight scattering out the empty doorways. The clouds of the day had broken up enough that he had the moon to guide him as he made his slow way back down the hill to a lit street, where he might find a palanquin and make his way home.

# 21

"Donier Jullavyr a Fieled of the third rank," he announced himself
at the entrance to the Afusel household. The servant ushered him
to a sitting room with a balcony that opened up onto a small
courtyard. At its center were three orange trees, and the sound of
children at play rang up through their leaves as they played.

He waited, fidgeting in a high-backed chair for a long time
before Liene ul Terainous was finally shown through the door by
the servant. She sat where he indicated in a chair nearly halfway
across the room from Donier, shrinking back into it. Donier shook
his head and picked his own chair up to move it closer to hers,
ignoring the frown of the servant. He settled it so that he was
within reach of her, and as he sat himself the image of his hand on
her knee while he consoled her glanced through his mind.

Donier waited, but no wine or drink of any sort was offered
him, the servant a disapproving presence. Both chairs, he noted,
were worn at the arms, and there was a smell about the room, even
with the windows thrown open, of dilapidation and must. Looking
closer, he saw that the curtains by the balcony were drab, and while
all the furniture was of great quality, the pieces were old and either
through lack of interest or money had begun to edge towards
disrepair.

"Good of you to see me, Nes Liene. I hope the day finds you
well," he said, clearing his throat as he spoke.

She nodded in a furtive way, her eyes flicking in the direction of
the servant. "I am well, thank you. To what do I owe this honor?"

"My concern for your welfare, of course. I can't imagine the anguish you must have suffered these last weeks with no word of Terainous at all."

"It has been difficult, I cannot deny," she said. It seemed she was about to say more, but she glanced away to the balcony, appearing to forget he was even there.

Donier waited a moment and then cleared his throat, wondering again why no drink was on offer. "I wanted to be sure that you knew that if there was anything I could do, you need only ask it of me."

Liene turned back to face him, smiling broadly. "Your friendship to Terainous meant more than you can know, and I am grateful for your offer. I will send to you if anything should come up."

"I am glad to hear that of my friend. He was a great and honorable man." He shook his head. "I suppose I should not be speaking of him as though he is dead. One never knows what the Gods have in store for any of us."

"No," she said, surprising him with a bitter laugh. "No, we cannot know."

He wet his lips, unsure how to respond. Liene was again staring out beyond the balcony. Looking at her he could see that her gaze went nowhere, was focused on nothing. He shifted uncomfortably in his chair, the frown of the servant seeming to grow deeper by the moment. The atmosphere with the servant and Liene and the decaying room around felt like one of mourning and death, and it made Donier want to shiver.

"I cannot leave," she said in the barest of whispers, "until they find Terainous. The Afusel will not return my dowry until they have proof of his death, so my family tells me to stay. To act as though he will return. You know he has passed to the Hall?"

It took him a moment to realize that was a question. "Yes," he said. "Whatever happened to him. He could not have survived the current."

She nodded, seeming to be excited, leaning forward in her chair. "You saw it. You saw it all."

"Yes."

She slumped back, despondent. "I just want to know. I just want to know."

"Yes."

"I asked the Gver at the Feast of Balance to send a search party, but I have heard nothing."

She said this last with such emotion that it gave him pause. He wondered at what was behind this, why this of all things would draw the most feeling from her, and recalled the scene he had witnessed from the feast night at the Gver's Palace. Had he thrown her aside without any regard after that night? The thought of her in the grasp of that fat fool.

"Would you be able to help with this?" she asked when she had regained herself. "Anything at all. I would be forever in your debt."

"Of course," he replied. "I will speak with Nes Ludenn. Perhaps he can speak with the Gver on this."

He made his excuses and left her to that place. On his way to the Afieled estates, which were much farther out from the palace, he stopped at an establishment for some wine to cleanse his throat, feeling as though he were spiting the Afusel servant even now. Two cups from a fine bottle could wash away the dread he felt. Sitting there, he had been overcome by the irrational thought that somehow he would be entrapped there as well, apiece with the furniture wearing away down through the years till he was faded and unrecognizable to all his companions.

Terainous had never spoken of the estate or his life there while they were together. All Donier knew was that he came from an important family, one that had suffered a gradual falling of prestige these last generations, but still a name that commanded respect. What Donier had just seen was an estate on the precipice of ruin, no longer able to maintain appearances. It explained why they might prefer to not accept the cohorts' verdict, for if Terainous were dead they would need to return Liene's dowry, and doing so might leave them utterly destitute. Such a thing would be unimaginable. What had happened to them?

He wished now that he had not gone to see her. Better not to know the lies Terainous had assumed; better to remember him as he had known him—a carefree man with a beautiful wife. He would go to her again, he knew it now. No matter the discomfort, he would not be able to stay away.

That night he dreamed of being lost in the desert. An endless vista of hard scrub and sun-blasted earth expanded in all directions from where he stood, bedraggled and tired. He looked at the soaring emptiness above, squinting against the sun, his hands fidgeting with his robes. There was no sound anywhere; not even the wind moved. He began to walk, going forward at random. Nothing came into view and the silence still held reign. His footsteps did not even stir dust from the ground.

# 22

Nazeed was the name of the man who met him at the drinkery where Osiphan had told him to wait. He was a short man, running to fat, and so unprepossessing that he was able to slide into the chair opposite Masiph's without his even noticing. After some wary introductions, Nazeed led him out of the drinkery to the edge of the district and a rundown establishment, The Adizad's Sword. They entered through the alley and went upstairs to one of the rooms. Nazeed indicated for him to sit in lone chair while he leaned against the windowsill.

Neither of them spoke as they waited, Maisph occupying himself in studying the wretched-looking bed that sat across from him. The door to the room next to them closed and the sound of two men in muffled conversation reached their ears. The talk ended quickly and was followed by grunts and moans and the scraping of furniture on the wood. Masiph glanced over at Nazeed, but his expression remained unchanged.

Masiph could feel sweat beginning to run down his back and he was sure his face was flushed. What, in ancestors' name, had he gotten himself into, he wondered. Was this the plan, to have him entrapped in such a place and be able to extort him or who knew what? He tried to gauge his chances of getting out the door and out of this place without incident, but he suspected the fat man could move much faster than appearances suggested.

He was in the pit of these swirling thoughts, unable to stop listening, and envisioning the scene next door, when the door swung open and a man in a plain gray robe stepped within. He walked to the center of the room and threw back the hood that shrouded his face, looking down at Masiph with a smile.

"I'd hoped you would come," Osiphan said, and he sat across from him on the bed. He gestured at the room. "I apologize for this, but sadly we can't have talks like this in the public realm. We all have a reason to be here, even if it is for a sodden touch."

Masiph didn't reply, his unease only growing by the moment, though now it was focused on the Husem sitting opposite him. The gravity of the path he had set himself was becoming apparent to him, and he wondered how he would be able to extricate himself from this should it become necessary.

"You've met one of us already," Osiphan continued, motioning at Nazeed. "There are a great many others, young Nohritai like you who have had to suffer the whims of a tyrant and his hatchetman. You'll have the chance to meet some of them soon, I hope."

"I hope so too," Masiph said, for lack of anything else to say.

This seemed to encourage the Husem. "I won't say much about what we are about. There will be plenty of time for that. I will just say that all of us share a common goal, common concerns. The empire has grown flaccid, emaciated, all power centered on the Ad Eselte and his small coterie while the rest of the Nohritai are little more than servants. When the Renuih were great, when our empire was at its largest, the Nohritai did not live at the sufferance of the Emperor. That is no coincidence."

Masiph swallowed as the groaning next door reached a crescendo. Osiphan waited for the noise to subside and then continued. "But you know all this as well as we do, I suspect. Why else would you be here, right?"

"I guess," Masiph said, clearing his throat. Why was he here?

"Of course it is. Of course it is. The way you have been treated is offensive to any self-respecting Nohritai. If something like this can happen to you, of all of us, none of us is safe. Nothing we have can be called our own and any talk of rights is a cruel joke. It cannot be allowed to stand.

"Think of it. We, whose loyalty to the Empire cannot be questioned, are forced to hide ourselves amidst this," he said, gesturing around them, "while the Empire abuses us in kind, taking us at all fours as if we are his gentlemen ushers."

Masiph nodded, afraid of saying anything more.

Osiphan smiled. "This is a difficult step we are asking you to take, but it is one I think you know you must. Still, it would be too much for me to expect you to make a decision right now, especially here of all places. So I will only ask that you think of what I have said. I'm sure you will see the righteousness of the cause and you will join us in our struggle."

"Very well."

"Good. Good. Nazeed will give you the details of the next meeting. He will be your contact to our group. You will understand that until we know that we can trust you, we cannot have you meeting many of the others. It would put us at too great a risk. For the same reason you and I will not meet again for a long time. But you will be in good hands with Nazeed. He speaks for me in all things."

Next door, the two men exited the room. As if that were some sort of signal, Osiphan too stood. "The choice is yours," he said as he flipped his hood over his head. "Do not think, though, that you can talk about this to any authorities. My word and my connections weigh far greater than yours. I'll have you whipped for perversion long before you'll have me wheeled for treason. Do not forget."

"I won't," Masiph said. He stood and they clasped arms formally and then Osiphan left, closing the door behind him.

Nazeed stood up from the windowsill. He told Masiph of a gathering a week from now in the Luithen District at a certain warehouse. He described the warehouse and the street and how Masiph was to enter it and the signal he should give before doing so. He should not dress as he normally did. With that and without any goodbyes, Nazeed sent Masiph out into the depths of the night. The first marks of daylight were forming along the horizon as he returned home.

He fell into his bed, not even bothering to remove his robes, the frenetic buzzing in his mind from what he had just involved himself in not enough to keep sleep at bay. As the sun rose, he dreamed. A tree grew from his loins, a desert tree, and from its roots the Eresnan flowed. Its canopy spread over the whole of old Renuih, the desert and the three kingdoms included. All manner of birds cried out above, some he had never heard before. A wind stirred the leaves in the trees, sharp as swords, and as they blew they pointed towards the ruined cities of the desert.

# THREE:

# THE REIGN OF THE IMPURE

# 23

There were five bodies already on display on the boards when the latest was brought in. The functionary straightened its clothes as best he could and then left it. They gave off a slightly singed odor. The corpse was that of a young man, trim and athletic, though somewhat short. His skin was a dark shade of red, suggesting that he originated in the western coastal regions, perhaps Nrai or Xln. There was nothing memorable about his features, though there was something of a knowing sneer in his expression, which might have been habitual. Nothing about the appearance of the body, or the poor state of the clothing on it, suggested anything about how the man had died.

The morgue was attached to the central Magisterium, just off The Hashil, the central boulevard that led from the nearby palace to the main gates of Lastl. A steady stream of visitors came to room throughout the day – relatives, or the curious seeking a glimpse of the unknowns. They were led in by a Magister who took them to the head of each board. Everyone entered with the same apprehensive expression, as if they weren't sure whether it was worse to find what they sought or to leave empty handed.

It was mostly men who came, brothers or fathers or perhaps uncles or cousins. If there was no one else, sometimes a wife or a mother would make a tear-filled appearance. They were all of the lesser classes, for if the magistery discovered a body of someone of the rank they did not place it in the public room. The only people of rank who passed through came for their own amusement, to gawk at the prostitutes and drunkards, and especially those who had come to a particularly grisly end.

The curious were disappointed by the six currently on display. One was an old beggar who had been found on the corner of Wussilen near the Ulternine cloister the morning before by one of the Cureders, who wondered why the man hadn't come in for the daily meal they gave him. He was on the board as a mere formality and in two days would be returned to the cloister for a pauper's burial. The other four were as unremarkable as the new corpse – just men who had seemingly led honorable lives but happened to die at an inopportune moment on the streets of Lastl, alone. Only one had a visible wound of any sort, a young man with the poor beginnings of a beard on him. He had taken a dagger through the ribs. The wound itself was not visible; only the place where his silks darkened with blood indicated that anything was amiss.

The corpse was displayed for three days, and by the third all its companions were different. The beggar had been properly buried and replaced by an aged whore who was missing a great many of her teeth. On his other side was someone who, by the cut of his clothes, had been a respectable merchant, who according to witnesses had simply walked into the Jenian River, still high and fast from the late spring rains, and had disappeared in its current. He had been caught up in the stevedores' ropes downstream. Oddly, the scorched fragrance that had marked him initially still hung about him, and stranger still there was not any stench of putrefaction, though it had been very hot and humid the last two days.

On the third evening a new body was brought in, leaving seven for display. By his shading he was a Lastl man, of indeterminate quality, though clearly not of rank. He had been discovered in an alley behind several taverns, where it was not uncommon for bodies of various sorts to end up, beaten rather badly and his throat slashed. An attempt had been made to mar his features as well, with his nose hacked off and his eyes gouged.

In the work to disfigure and render anonymous the corpse, his killer or killers hadn't noticed the mark on his hand, dark like a mole, and shaped, some said, like a man bent over. It was this mark which his wife found when she came in to the viewing room the next day and identified him. "I just knew something was wrong," she repeated to the Magister, who completed the report and helped her arrange the transfer of the body to her local cloister. Having got the woman and her brother on their way, the Magister called one of the underlings and sent him off to the palace to notify them that one of their guard would not be reporting for duty any longer.

It had been Tehh's idea. "We have nothing to lose by it," he declared. Perhaps something to gain, if they were fortunate. They had not been. Instead, one of the palace guard had turned up, which seemed too much a coincidence.

Although they hadn't managed to get anywhere in terms of determining the identity of the assassin, they had been successful at keeping the incident under wraps. Cepedutherupt had recovered quickly, as Adepts seemed to, and had started his journey back to the capital two days later. That same day, having heard not so much as a whisper about the assassination attempt in the city, Tehh decided to send the assassin's body to the morgue for display.

No one had questioned the High Adept's presence in the palace, nor the fact that he had come unannounced but left with full ceremony, led down The Hashil by the Master of Gates. That Cepedutherupt should appear without explanation in the palace confirmed what everyone already apparently believed, which was that he and Keleprai were plotting the course of the Realm together.

Keleprai had been unable to sleep for the better part of the last four nights since the attack. When he had slept it had been disturbed. He would start awake, an hour or minutes after he slipped off, drenched in sweat, the smell of the assassin in his death throes somehow in his nostrils. Days he was fine. His guard was increased and everyone put on alert. If an attack was to come, he thought, let it come. Whatever self lay beneath him in those moments when sleep beckoned and seized him felt differently. That would pass, though, he knew.

He had spent the morning in audiences with various nobles of the lesser ranks and had developed a headache for his troubles. He thought longingly of mythres or perhaps some wine – anything that might blot out the tediousness of who had hunting rights over this particular stand of trees, or whether a dowry had been properly dealt with by the receiving family. He was going to spend his afternoon being petitioned by various Officers of the City for funds and planning for projects. First, though, he had to be updated on the investigation into the attack by Adept Tehh.

"The guard's name was Fennen," the Adept said as Keleprai entered, not even waiting for him to sit. The smell of musty tomes and dust was overwhelming, even in this outer room. Sometimes Keleprai thought all the books and scrolls of Craitol could be found scattered within the old man's quarters.

"He had sizable debts that he owed to Morning. Not a keen eye for the match, I'm afraid."

Keleprai managed to find a seat free of clutter, and deposited himself in it. "What do you mean by sizable?"

Tehh shrugged. "Large enough that his wife knew about them. Not so large to be killed for, I would think, but large enough."

"This is our man."

"Undoubtedly. His face, so I am told, was cut beyond all recognition. Fortunately, his wife was able to identify him still."

Keleprai nodded. "And now."

Tehh waved a hand at him. "I've sent my Disciple to see what he can find. He is working with the Magistery. It will take some time, I'd imagine. They won't be forthcoming."

"Hardly. If Morning is involved, though, I expect we can assume who else is."

The Adept did not respond except to give him a look: *Of course.* The Adyriessen had connections to Morning. They had feuded with the Alastl since his father had chosen a family from Takyl above them to provide the wife of his son. This was the usual nonsense then, though the engine they had found in the passway suggested otherwise.

"Why would be the next question," the Adept said. "That is not so easily divined."

Keleprai did not reply. This past winter an official from Tuin, related to the Apysel in some manner, had been murdered outside a brothel known to specialize in males, while on a trade mission to the city. That had led to a series of attacks on minor Alastl officials throughout the season, with his people responding in kind. He remained absolutely certain that the Adryssien were behind the initial killing. The feud had quieted with the arrival of spring, and likely by winter would be forgotten, replaced by new grievances and further blood.

"I have no idea why they would want an escalation like this. And the engine. I had not thought any of the families would turn to them."

Tehh shrugged. "A diversion, perhaps. Let's see what we find. Likely there is more to come. These things always spiral deeper and deeper the further in you go."

They finished soon after and Keleprai left the Adept to his mustiness and his ink. These things always spiraled deeper, it was true. The Adyrissen and the Morning would never act alone in something of this gravity, not an attack against the Gver himself involving an assassin using a blasphemous alkemycal practice. They hadn't discussed it, and he supposed it was within the realm of possibility that drawings still existed somewhere and that somehow the conspirators had gained them, but far more likely was that one of the four people who knew the passages of this palace had tried to have him killed.

# 24

It was a strange realm the riverboat passed as it moved upriver at a
stately pace, propelled by a galley of slaves chained to their oars.
They were out of sight, the only reminder of their existence the
steady, hypnotic pulling of the oars against the current and the odd
bellow of the galley master that reached to the deck. The air was
hazy from the heat, so heavy that the woolen robes Vyissan was
wearing constantly felt damp. There was little jungle around the
river, but what there was had garishly colored leaves and flowers,
so unlike any forest in the west. The cities and towns they passed,
as with Sylaron and Hessen, looked very much like any Craitolian
city. That was hardly surprising given that most of those had been
modeled after Renian cities. Lastl and Takyl had in fact been
Imperial cities, the farthest west the Empire had ever reached. It
was only on closer inspection that the differences became obvious:
blue houses instead of red, the grand-domed mausoleums to their
dead, and the profusion of vegetation that seemed to threaten the
sanctity of every street.

The river itself was its own dominion, a shifting terrain of
vessels, all manner and trade. The boat he was on was a passenger
ferry that ran from Darrhynn south to Sylaron and north again,
stopping at cities and towns along the way, at least one a day to set
anchor for the night. There were around two dozen other
passengers on the ship, a shifting mixture of merchants and minor
Nohritai. A smaller vessel followed in tow, where some of the
servants and crew would spend the nights and where the swords,

hired for the trip, would spend the days, only coming onto the main ship at night to stand watch. The main vessel had the feeling of a pleasure cruise, for there were no women aboard, and the men left to their own devices turned to drinking and gaming throughout the day. They would all disembark each evening at whatever town they were staying in and head for an inn near the shore that made all its business from such vessels.

Vyissan stayed to himself mostly, a difficult thing on such a small boat, making a show of sketching the passing countryside. In reality he was taking extensive notes on all he saw of the realm, the cities and towns and their populace, the commerce he saw passing along the river, the industry he noticed in towns, and any vegetation or animals he thought remarkable.

Of that there was much, though in truth the sight which still remained foremost in his mind were the ruins he had discovered during his passage through the desert. One of the swords had stumbled over the foundation, what remained of it, of a building while wandering off the road on one of their stops. When he had told the rest of them of it Vyissan had gone to investigate. Some cursory digging revealed the shards of a great city scattered along an empty floodplain, the river that had flowed there long vanished. There was little left of the ruins but crumbled foundations here and there overgrown with sage. Whatever order had existed was lost to the desert and he could not tell what any of the buildings might have been.

"These were before the highway," Inahan said when Vyissan asked if there was a lost Imperial city he was unaware of. "Long before, I should say. I've never seen this type of material used in an Imperial city anywhere before."

"Nor I," Vyissan agreed. The stone was the color of the desert, and perhaps it had been made of the earth there somehow, though he could not have said. None of the others knew anything of the provenance of the ruins, with Inahan saying he knew of no people having been in this part of the desert before the Renuiha. The ruins, the very foreignness of stone and the foundations it formed, suggested otherwise.

Vyissan made them stop while he tramped across both sides of the road to inspect the various foundations and random groupings of stone, all worn smooth by the wind. It stunned him to think that there had been a people here before the Renuiha, before the Enir.

He supposed it shouldn't have – after all, the Mgetir had been in the south of Craitol before the Craitolians had taken it from them and the Kragians had followed the Craitolians south, crossing the wastelands centuries later. But that was all known. All he knew, and all these men knew, were that the Renians, of which they were all descendant, had held the desert and beyond west long before the Craitolians had come south. Only the arrival of the Shadow Men had ended their reign. And yet here was something outside history, outside of all knowledge, that mocked what they understood of the past and existence. For if these people, whoever they had been, could simply vanish leaving nothing but broken stone...

That thought troubled him still, though he could not say why. Empires were broken and Qrauls overthrown in a moment, he knew this. Perhaps it was simply the tediousness of the journey now that he was in Renuih and heading upriver, which left him with nothing else but to sketch and map the river course and dwell within his thoughts. He had never sat easily with nobility or the wealthy, and this was no different. The Renians treated him with the same distance that the Craitolians did, though in this case it was his beard that marked him not his shade.

The sight of those broken remains of the disappeared stirred an overwhelming emotion in him. He had not felt the like since in the days before he had set out on this quest when he had gone to the Cureders at the cloister for Melinon. They had drawn some blood from his wrist into a pan and set it upon a fire to burn. Then, from the scalded pattern, they had prophesied his future. The rush he had felt watching his blood dripping from the shallow wound, the exultation that here would be realized some form of truth, was matched by the sense of doom that had come over him in that place where the emptiness of the desert marked an absence.

The conversation on the ship was dull, mostly tedious gossip, meaningless to Vyissan, serving only to drag out the uneventful hours. These were minor Nohritai and merchants, of little worth in the large part, and their concerns were decidedly inconsequential as well. The only thing of value he managed to extract from his few conversations in the first days of the journey was that the Shadows had raided Darrhyn earlier that summer. Such a thing was unheard of, and though it appeared nothing of consequence had actually befallen the first city, the blow was still resounding in the minds of the Renuiha. Never had they conceived of such a thing occurring.

"They are planning an invasion, I am sure of it," one man said. "The raid on Darrhyn was to place their agents in the city, and when they are ready they shall strike at all the Great Families."

That seemed like nonsense to Vyissan – the Shadow Men hardly seemed interested, let alone capable, of such intrigue. He wondered if the stultifying heat of this river and its environs had a deleterious effect on the Renian mind. It sometimes seemed as though it did on him; every day he grew more sluggish, moving about the boat as slowly as it plied the waters.

What were they, these Shadows? No one knew to say with any certainty. They wandered the desert, unseen mostly, yet looming in the minds of any who lived near. It was easy to say that they were little better than vermin, acting without reason but for their need to plunder and kill. What did they do but wreak destruction and wander in search of their next victims? But that bothered him somehow, just as the ruins in the desert had, for there were lives there, no matter that they were lived beyond civilization.

The Shadows must have love and laughter, sadness and hate, no matter how base. There was a slander visited upon his kind, the Kragians, calling them the mirror to the Shadow Men, their pallor marking the same absence that the Shadow's darkness did. The stain of imperfection visited upon them both by the Gods. What fools they were, he thought, to presume to know anything about one another. They were all tolotes spied in the distance just along the horizon, visible with the bouncing of the tail, and then a moment later gone.

One of the other passengers, a trader from Estuen, took an interest in him in spite of his attempts to keep himself apart from his fellow travelers. He had come aboard in Sylaron with Vyissan and they had talked briefly then, the merchant pressing him for information on his purpose in Renuih. That had put Vyissan immediately on his guard and his response had been polite but curt, a merchant keeping his business in the folds of his robes and nothing more. The man had let him be then, but Vyissan had looked around from his sketching several times to find the man studying him from one vantage point or another.

On the third day, as though he had needed some time to muster the courage, he approached Vyissan again as he settled down to sketch in the shade of the boat's stern.

"Where do your ancestors lie, friend?" he said, leaning against the ship's railing and looking down at Vyissan's papers.

"Tuissar," Vyissan said, turning the papers over in his lap.

"A grand city. A grand city. I'm from Estuen. A mote and a speck by comparison."

"So you said."

"Yes, yes. I'm Gethuul." He smiled and Vyissan smiled in return, not offering his own name.

"Well, friend," he said when it was clear Vyissan would not say anything, "where does your drawing take you?"

"I'm just passing the days."

"Good, good. Never had the hand for it. Or the eye, I suppose." Another pause hung between them before Gethuul leapt to strike it down. "What is your trade then, friend?"

"Much the same as yours I suppose," Vyissan said, wondering how true that might be. He did not think he had been followed in Sylaron, but it was possible he had been noticed, especially after his incident on the street. It was also likely that Imperial agents regularly traveled up and down the river to watch for men such as him. The Qraul's agents did much the same thing in Craitol, especially in the north, as he well knew.

"Much the same," Gethuul said, as though Vyissan had made a joke. "Yes, friend, I suppose we are in the same trade. For your sake, I hope not."

"And why is that?"

"I don't think I need to draw it out for you. Yours is the hand for that, after all. I just hope your destination is not much farther up river."

"I can't imagine our paths crossing."

Gethuul chuckled, shaking his head, and then leaned in closer so that his eyes were level with Vyissan's. "No, I imagine you can't, but I know your kind, friend. I know it. Hiding behind your beard, hands in your robes. Grasping a coin, no doubt. No, I know your kind. Just know that I am watching you."

Vyissan nodded and the merchant walked away to the center of the vessel, where they were setting up to play the day's first hand of cards.

What in the Gods' sacred names had that been about, he wondered. He was familiar with that tone, enraged by it. How many Craitolians had used it when speaking to him? Even so, why would a merchant from Estuen, a speck in the Empire after all, be concerned with the travels of a modest Enir trader? What did it matter to him if he went to Darrhyn, home to a thousand other Enir? It did not stand to reason. How laughable, he thought, that his disguise would work so well as to draw the suspicions of the authorities who saw a spy in every Enir trader.

It worried him what the man might do. Would he be able to incite the other passengers to some kind of violence? The thought of having to deal with that both exhausted and frightened him. Why not get off this boat at the next port, Vyissan thought, and wander wherever his whim called him, just another Enir in the empire? There was nothing to stop him. He could imagine an entire life unspooling from that single choice, an itinerant life, town to village to city, and perhaps, if the Gods allowed, an opportunity to settle in a place for a time. He would never do it, of course. This burden was his to see through.

# 25

Masiph had been told little, and trusted with less, the first two meetings Nazeed had organized with him. They were tests, those encounters – attempts to divine his intentions. Two others had joined them both times, a boy whose name Masiph could not recall, and Lisser, a man of Nazeed's vintage, clearly a Nohritai by his bearing. He was a frowning, stern presence looking over their proceedings as though judging every word spoken, while the boy and Nazeed engaged Masiph in discussions on the state of the Empire. He had been careful in everything he said, refusing to be baited into saying anything treasonous, but not disagreeing exactly with anything they said. It appeared that Lisser approved of him, though, for last night, when he had been walking home deep in the bowels of the evening after a chew and some drinks, Nazeed had appeared at his side and taken him to another drinkery.

From the street it looked closed, but they were admitted after Nazeed administered a sharp double-knock to the door. The place was empty but for them, with only a few lanterns still on near the bar and kitchen, where the man who let them in immediately retreated. Nazeed poured them both a drink from one of the casks and then they sat well out of hearing of the man, just beyond the circle of light from the lamps, and Masiph was told what was required of him.

The details were clear and he was clever enough not to ask many questions. Now he was in Asan, a public chewing room, sitting at a table that could be seen from the street, as he had been told . He ordered a chew and was working it over in his mouth with an eye on the passersby in the street when a man slid into the seat across from him.

"Husem Gelluhel?" the man asked, as Nazeed had said he would. He was a nondescript figure, a thin face with small darting eyes and unruly hair.

"Yes."

The man nodded and pushed a package across the table to him. It had been wrapped to look like a gift to a woman, in the finest paper, painted with birds. Within was what would appear to be a porcelain figure of a nahyren bird. He picked it up, pretending to study it, testing its weight in his hand. The paper he saw was marked with a few lines from a poem he did not recognize: *The nahyren alights, the silence is whole.* It was larger and heavier than most such figurines he had seen, but otherwise unremarkable.

"It is to your satisfaction?"

"Most certainly."

They talked a bit about the quality of the aslyn at the Asan. The man recommended a particular chew with dala beans in it, which Masiph had not tried. Then he left with a nod, disappearing into the crowd. Masiph waited a while, finishing his chew, and then he too left, making his way to Isinan and the Imperial Palace.

He walked with a purpose, not wanting to get caught in a shower and have the paper wrapping damaged. It was morning, but the sky was already dark with the clouds of a gathering storm. He was damp from the humidity and his own anxiety, so he made sure to hold the package by the strings to ensure that his sweat would not stain the paper. There would be no problems, Nazeed had assured him. If the guards at the palace questioned him about why he had it with him, he was to act embarrassed and stammer a bit. A young scamp at play.

For a while he was certain he was being followed and he went off Isinan, doubling back down another street. He didn't notice anyone following his path, but he still could not shake the feeling. Dahrryn mirrored his state of mind, had for several days now. Everyone seemed to be whispering to one another and looking at passing strangers with suspicion. The shadows in every corner were ominous.

Word had come three or four days ago of a Shadow Men raid on Eles, a northern city. It was a smaller center and had been the subject of attacks before, but this had involved a larger force than usual, which had overwhelmed the city guard on the walls and managed to loot the city's granary and a few merchant warehouses. The force had then turned farther north and laid waste to the countryside, burning all the villages and crops in its path before returning across the river to the desert. This, combined with three other recent attacks, none of them as large, had the capital convulsed in paroxysms of worry.

There were astounding rumors everywhere – Masiph had heard them in the chewing room that morning and in the drinkery the night before – of a vast conspiracy involving the Shadows. Even the eunuchs in the household were whispering of it. The Emperor, it was said, had called the High Nohritai to discuss a war of some kind against the Shadow Men. They had refused to support such an action, because their ranks had been infiltrated by the Shadows who had invaded the capital. In the coming days there would be a signal sent from the desert to have these hidden conspirators murder the Nohritai in their midst and open the city gates to the desert horde. The Shadows were all Adepts, skilled in alkemya, and able to impersonate anyone if the stories were to be credited. It was hard to believe, he thought, that anyone could give them credence, yet half the populace seemed to be speaking of nothing else.

The guards gave him no more than a cursory glance at the palace gates once he had announced himself and his intentions. It surprised him, though Nazeed had been sure there would no trouble.

"What is strange about the son of the Vazeir going to see his father?" he had said.

"But I've never done it before. Only when he has set an audience."

Nazeed had shrugged. "How would they know that?"

Neither of the suliher looked at the figurine, nor did they question what his business with his father might be. There was none of the ceremony that had attended his last visit. No Ceinobyte waited to bless him as he passed through the second gate, and there was no courtier to guide him once he was through. The heralds at the gates stayed silent as he passed. He went along the same path as before, noticing this time how how carefully it had all been designed. One could walk along here and not see any of the buildings of the outer courtyard, where most of the administration of government took place and where all the functionaries of the court lived, but the six domes of the Imperial Palace were visible with each step.

He did not stay on the main path for long, cutting off on one of its branches before he reached the inner wall. He crossed a bridge, and the stream that it went over seemed to mark the border between the Imperial way and the more profane parts of the palace grounds. While he did so, the bells rang, signaling midday. There were streets of a sort and he could see various official-looking buildings, what he thought were the justice and treasury buildings, perhaps the library. It had been years since he had been here. The largest, he knew, was the Vazeir's Palace, though he could not see that yet for it was actually behind the palace closing the circle the outer courtyard made around the inner courtyard.

"Ad Ezern." The cry caused him to break stride and look about. Just emerging from one of the buildings—the engineering offices?—was the courtier who had led him to his audience. Masiph swore under his breath and waved in reply.

The courtier rushed up to him, slightly out of breath. "What luck seeing you here, Most Gracious."

Masiph nodded gravely, trying and failing to recall the man's name. He did not appear to notice, hurrying on. "What a glorious day that was. I think of it still. I'm certain, Husem Masiph, that I will be telling my children, should my ancestors so bless me, of the day I witnessed the elevation of Husem Masiph id Ezern to Suliher."

"Thank you," Masiph said in an abrupt tone, hoping to discourage him. The courtier ignored him and asked what he was doing at the Imperial Palace. Masiph saw his eyes light up when he told him that he was there to see his father, and he resisted the urge to swear again.

"Such a wonderful man. I had the chance to meet him on two occasions. His service to Ad Eselte and the Empire is unmatched. It would be so humbling to work for such a man, I imagine."

Did this provincial fool, Masiph wondered, know nothing of the family history? Had he managed to somehow escape all the gossip about the relations between the Ezern father and son? Or was he simply so grasping as not to care? Masiph did not have time for this. The man he was to meet would wait no more than a quarter of an hour after the noon bell for the exchange.

The courtier began to tell him of the first time he had been in the exalted presence of the magnificent Ibrazol. Masiph cut him off with a smile. "I'm terribly sorry, but my father does not have much time to spare me, you understand. I must be on my way. I will mention your admiration to him."

The courtier was ecstatic at his words, offering him unending expressions of thanks as Masiph walked away nodding goodbye. For a moment he thought the man was going to follow him all the way to the doors of the Vazeir's Palace, but he finally waved his farewell and wandered off. Masiph darted away down the street, head down, hoping to avoid any further encounters. Chance was kind to him, and he saw no one else as he passed a few unremarkable buildings.

The flow of traffic began to ease, and it dwindled further as he left the buildings behind and entered another gardened area, intended to evoke the plains to the east of the capital, with short, hardy trees and scrub. The outer wall towered above the vegetation, and nestled against it was a small shrine. He made his way towards it, glancing behind him to see if any others were on the same path. There were none and he slipped within, ducking his head as he did so, as though he suspected someone of watching him.

The shrine was larger than it appeared and its inner sanctums were substantial. The entire structure was open to the elements, as most such shrines were. He went into the nearest sanctum as he had been instructed. It was a spartan place, as they all seemed to be, the floor bare so that one might prostrate oneself in contemplation. There was a slanted half-roof creeping up the sides of the walls to keep out the worst of the rain. Along each side of the long room were small shrines where one might place a gift or light a candle.

He went to the nearest and lit a candle. There was a statuette of some individual, a courtier by the dress that had been put upon it, prostrated, eyes downcast in the presence of the holy Emperor. There were a few coins and other objects scattered amongst the candles, a cheaply jeweled display dagger, and a quality stylus. Masiph glanced down at the wrapped figurine and wondered what one of the Ceinobytes might think of such an absurd offering. It was not something that one should be giving at any shrine or mausoleum, except perhaps one's mother or grandmother, but especially not at a shrine dedicated to the functionaries of the empire.

Having lit the candle, he stood for a moment, staring at it and the prostrated figure before him. His back began to itch with sweat.

"Not a day for contemplation." Those were the words he had been told to wait for.

"No," he replied, turning to face the newcomer, and was surprised to see it was one of the Ceinobytes of the shrine, his arms folded across his chest, each hand hidden in the sleeves of his drab green robe.

"You live in grace," the Ceinobyte intoned as he stepped forward, drawing his arms out from his sleeves and taking the figurine from Masiph. He stepped around him to the shrine and gathered the knife and the stylus as well. Masiph watched him, hesitating.

"Ancestors guard you," the Ceinobyte said. Masiph nodded in reply and walked stiffly out of the room and back to the main road. Only when he was well along his way, back in amongst the crowds of courtiers and attendants moving among the administrative buildings, did he begin to relax. The tension which had knotted in his stomach let out and he almost laughed with joy. He wanted to grab one of these passersby and tell him of his exploits.

He went to see his father as planned so that later, should it come to that, he would have an explanation for being on the palace grounds. It would not, he was sure, but he wanted to go anyway, to sit before the man, his act of defiance still fresh in the doing. When the attendant ushered him into the audience chamber, Masiph could see that Ibrazol was taken aback. He drew a measure of satisfaction from that.

"What brings you this way?" Ibrazol asked his son after they had concluded their greetings. He grimaced fleetingly as he said it. They had the same narrow face and large eyes, the same thin, ragged hair, though on Ibrazol it had receded well back on his forehead. They were even the same height, though Masiph still looked like a boy standing next to him, shallow chested and unmuscled. More than size, though, his father had a presence, a coiled, contained energy. Masiph felt empty by comparison.

He shrugged slightly in response, as though he had just happened to be around. The giddiness he had initially felt upon entering ground away by his immediate anxiety at the encounter.

"I have audiences I must attend to." A slight rise of one eyebrow. "If you have something to say, speak it."

"I was wondering about my elevation." Masiph felt a sick kind of elation. *There, it has been said.*

Ibrazol's expression did not change. "That is not my decision."

"Yes, but I thought—"

He did not finish. Ibrazol held up a hand. "Do not ask me. It is not my decision. It was not my decision to make you a jetthir of the army, nor will it be my decision to elevate you. You must have patience that Husem Gheyuth and the Ad Eselte have your best interests and that of the Empire in mind."

He frowned as he said it, looking directly at Masiph, who felt a brief surge of terror under that gaze. Had he seen through him at a glance? Or was he thinking of Khibar who, through his own efforts, had elevated himself to second to the Vazeir of a province and who would never have thought to come to his uncle for a good word? He fought the urge to look away at something, anything other than his father's eyes.

"Was that all?" It was a dismissal, not a question. Masiph could see that Ibrazol had stopped paying attention to him already, thinking about what was next in his day. He stood and thanked his father for the audience.

Outside the audience chamber was a suliher, a jetthir, not many years older than himself. The soldier stepped forward and bowed his head as to an equal.

"Husem Masiph den Ibrazol."

Masiph inclined his head and the jetthir said, "I am Aths id Negurein. I have known your father for some time, so it is a great pleasure to finally meet his son. Your service to the city was exemplary."

Masiph shrugged awkwardly. He always felt like a liar discussing the raid and what he had done – most of that evening was still a jumble of half-remembered moments he had failed to assemble.

"I was glad for the opportunity," he said at last. He regretted it, wondering if the jetthir would realize his true meaning. But Aths smiled and nodded. They clasped arms and the jetthir was ushered into the audience chamber. Masiph caught a glance of his father striding forward to greet the newcomer, and then the door was closed.

# 26

It had been raining on and off throughout the morning, a band of
dark, heavy clouds settling over the city. For the moment it had
halted, though there was a slight mist in the air. A miserable day,
biting, with the wind and a damp that rotted at the bone. Disciple
Hieran tramped, disgusted, through the streets to the Morning
grounds, his foul mood made worse by the sight of two palanquins
passing him on the road. He should have been used to it by now,
but it still galled him that the Disciple of the Adept of Lastl did not
have the coin to afford a rented palanquin in the rain. He cursed,
not the first time, the Council for joining him to the greatest miser
in the Realm. Not just a miser but a doddering old fool, more
interested in his scrolls and specimens than the alkemyc arts. So,
rather than practicing the art for which he had suffered years of
training and disappointments, Hieran spent his days as the Adept's
errand boy.

No, it had all been disappointment and dreams denied since he
had come, a supplicant, to the Council eight years ago. He had
barely been a man then, though he was already a thaumaturge of
some repute in his village Quilran, near Takyl. People came from
villages over two days' journey away just to have him heal their
broken bones and the like. Unaware that there were men such as
he in villages across the Realm, though few who were prodigies in
thaumaturgy as he was, Hieran got it into his head that he should
appeal to the Council to join their ranks.

And so, at fifteen, he had set out from home for Craitol, the

Qraul's city, to plead his case before the Council of Adepts. It was a harrowing journey for one who had hardly gone more than a day or so from Quilran. He spent a night in Takyl and was robbed and beaten and then spent another week on the streets of the city, begging for food and trying to find someone who would pay for his skills. When he had gained what he thought was enough coin for the journey he left Takyl, setting out for Craitol. His first two nights he spent at the roadside inns eating and drinking his fill and taking a girl to his room, only to find that his funds were nearly exhausted and the opportunities to earn more, which he had foolishly assumed would be there, were nonexistent. The rest of his journey he spent his nights in ditches under Senteur's heavens and even had to spend two days outdoors in Craitol itself until he managed to convince the gatekeepers at the Council's school that he was not some mere vagrant.

Fours years as a pupil passed with rigorous study of alkemya and its related arts. When he was deemed ready for elevation of rank, he submitted himself to the Council for testing, a grueling two-day affair where he had to demonstrate his abilities at drawing forth the astral aspects of various elements and shaping them into seeds of alkemy. He was judged to be of the highest proficiency and was admitted to the Council's inner circle, though they felt him lacking in some critical faculties and so named him a Disciple rather than an Adept. He should have been happy, for most who passed the tests—and there were many who did not—were left to the Council's outer circle to pass their days as unjoined conjurors, little grander in the scheme of things than a village thaumaturge. But instead, he was crushed by his failure to be named an Adept, a loss made all the keener by his joining to the Adept of Lastl. That hurt had not been lessened by the passage of time, mostly because his master Tehh was a man he thoroughly despised. And he had to suffer to submit, all his skill, the very astral of his being, to the service of that man, never his to be the guiding hand.

The Morning Grounds were not far from the palace and the coliseum. Nearest the street was the public match ground and attached to it were the Morning's betting and performing halls. Beyond that, and behind a wall, were the barracks and training fields for the players and a larger performing hall where the Morning's musicians, actors, and dancers would put on their grander performances. There was a match set for the afternoon, the Morning's third rank against Midday's, which was the reason Hieran had to suffer the rain. He praised the Gods that he would not have to endure the stands.

He went to the wagering hall, which was empty but for a few bettors and the usual hangers-on, stopping first at a stand near the entrance to buy a dala drink to warm himself, before beginning to wander around. He didn't have long to wait – a bookmaker approached him almost immediately. The man was short and a little stout, with a mess of hair that was starting to thin. His face was guarded in the way all such men were and he nodded a greeting at Hieran, which he returned in kind, neither of them particularly caring for the other's name.

"What have you?" Hieran asked.

The bookmaker shrugged noncommittally. "Depends, depends. Suppose you're looking for some asyl. I know some people who have dealings with some Enir traders. Long story, but they just got their latest supply last week. Very good quality, you cannot find its like in this city. You're a man of quality, I can see."

"Quite," the Disciple said. "That's not what I'm interested in today, though. I'm wondering about the odds for today's match. I've heard one of your stringers has gone missing."

A merest shrug of the shoulders. *How am I to keep track of the comings and goings of these players?*

"They probably don't have a replacement just yet, he only went yesterday."

The bookmaker waved his hand, "Pssh. He wasn't much of a player, you know. Could hardly manage a toss. He wasn't moving up the rankings, surely. No one's going to notice him missing, I can assure you of that.

"No, no sense throwing money after this today. There's no coin here," he said, gesturing about the hall. "Besides, it's going to be raining all day. Who wants to be sitting out in that? Now I have to, mind you, but I certainly don't encourage such behavior. No, your coin is better spent elsewhere. I happen to have the acquaintance of a few of the finer dancers of the Morning who will most certainly be free this afternoon. Why pay market price in the arches when a finer commodity is on offer and at fair coin?"

"Quality again."

"Indeed. Fair coin for fair coin."

"Sadly, I am on official business."

"Aren't we all."

Hieran smiled slightly. "From the Palace."

The bookmaker went silent, frowning. Hieran increased his smile. "You wouldn't happen to know a gentleman named Fennen? A Morning supporter."

"He was around," the bookmaker said.

"He was a palace guard," the Disciple said, followed by a shrug from the bookmaker. *What of it?*

"He was killed yesterday, in the alley of one of the Morning drinkeries. You probably heard. His face was disfigured."

Another shrug, though Hieran thought he detected some nervousness about the man. The wrong answer was now a dangerous proposition. If people were having palace guards murdered they would not hesitate to do the same to an odds man.

"He owed you money," Hieran said, gesturing to the betting hall. "A great deal of money, am I correct?"

"I wouldn't know. I didn't take his bets."

Hieran stared hard at the man, waiting. "I wouldn't know," he repeated.

"I am not a Magistery, obviously, but I do have the authority of the Gver to arrest you."

"On what basis?" the bookmaker demanded. It was Hieran's turn to shrug. *What did it matter?* He did not take his eyes from the bookmaker's.

"He has no debts with us," the bookmaker said at last.

Hieran let out a silent *Ah*. "How were they settled?"

The bookmaker had turned to stone, not even blinking. He did not answer.

Coincidences and more coincidences, all very convenient. Fennen's debts gone though not paid, and he murdered. A no-rank ball player vanishes at the same time and no one knows a thing about him past or future. In fact, no one knew anything – how long he had been with the Morning in Lastl, who he had spent time with, what he had done.

He had wandered through the betting hall and then over to the theater where some actors were running lines for that afternoon's performance and received much the same response. Everyone knew who he was speaking of, but whether they knew what had happened to him or not, they kept silent. A series of shrugs and avoided glances was all he got in return for his questions. How thick they all were.

It was to be expected, of course, and no one had bothered with coming up with a lie yet, which suggested that they did not attach any real importance to the man's disappearance. They simply saw no need to cooperate with one of the Gver's men. It was not unheard of for a stringer to vanish without reason. They hardly made enough to keep themselves in food, and at some point most were forced to admit that they were not going to rise through the ranks. A merchant wanting to have his rivals good stolen or anyone looking to have some brutality done to someone would come looking for just such a man, and if the money was good enough, well, why bother coming back?

He went into one of the barracks and began speaking to a hungover stringer, having talked his way past the gatekeepers and into the compound. The player's face was such an ashen color that Hieran felt ill just looking at him. He wasn't getting much out of the fellow beyond grunts and "Lazul was a good sort," so he decided to press on and see who else he could find that might volunteer more, or at least let something slip. He was met at the door by two hired swords, northerners by the look of them, who blocked his way with their short blades.

"I am from the Palace," he told them as though unfurling a passkey.

They did not reply, one of them simply stepping aside to allow him room to pass, jerking his head as he did so. Hieran considered arguing the point but decided against it and allowed himself to be led outside. The two swords walked on either side of him, neither bothering to sheath their swords, leading him along a path deeper into the Morning grounds. They were given a wide berth by everyone they passed, which was disconcerting, and he was taken to what he assumed was the estate of the Morning Chair. It was a sprawling building, three storied, with balconies and what looked like some walled gardens behind.

A servant let them in, observing their passage without expression. Panic seized Hieran once he realized that they were not going to throw him off the grounds. Instead they led him downstairs past the wine cellar, and through another basement before coming through a door to a cell. They stopped and one of the men unlocked the door while the other leveled his sword at

Hieran. He glanced about, trying to get what bearings he could in the gloom. The smell of earth was heavy in the air.

Once the door was open, the man gestured with his sword for Hieran to enter to the cell. He almost refused, ready to make his stand there, but thought better of it. It wasn't like they would kill him; the Chair of Morning could not afford to defy the Gver in such a way. The whole situation was bizarre. Why, if he was on the right track, draw such attention by imprisoning the Gver's representative?

Stepping into the cell, he started to say, "This is outrageous, you understand," and then one of them struck him hard on the back of the head. He fell to the floor with a grunt. Another blow and he felt as though he were floating atop an ebbing tide. He tried to look up at his attackers but he had no sense of whether he was actually moving his head or not. All he could see were waves of color that swirled across his vision. Another blow and the colors went, the gloom descending to dark

# 27

Nustef changed into his finest uniform, the one he used on days when there was an inspection. The undershirt was fine green ardeh wool, as were the leggings, while the robe was Craitolian silk, and the blue of the Watch. He wrapped and belted it carefully so that it was tight to his body, the collar open at the neck. The sleeves were voluminous, which marked him as a Nohritai, as did the length of the robe, which went almost to his ankles. He had his ceremonial dagger on his left side. His hat was of Watch color as well—a simple thing, the most expensive he could afford.

Erise watched him dress, a slight frown on her face. Seeing it, Nustef said, "He is not what you think he is."

Though she had never met Masiph, she had always harbored a distate for the youth. Nustef had felt the same way when he had been passed over for promotion to jetthir in favor of the Ad Ezern with no experience in the ranks. Everyone in the quadra had sneered at the news of another wayward son of a great family being given a fat rank where he could dabble without risk or consequence.

Masiph had fit the cliché his first month: arrogant and demanding without cause, with an expectation of success and praise where none had been earned. He had been humbled by the lack of reverence the quadra afforded him, and he had worked hard in turn, which had impressed Nustef. Slowly they had become friends, as Nustef became the only man in the quadra that the jetthir would trust enough to confide in. As he always told Erise, it never hurt to be on speaking terms with the son of the Vazeir of Darrhyn.

146

Erise had disagreed. "He needs you now," she had said to him a few months ago, "but what happens when he has moved on to whatever position his father finds for him next? Then he will need someone else of lower quality and you will not hear from him. He will not think of you."

And the truth of the matter was that since Masiph's coronation, Nustef had heard little from him. He had begun to harbor some doubts himself, but these he did not voice to his wife. That morning, though, one of the Ad Ezern eunuchs had come, requesting that he join Masiph in a chew that afternoon. The formality of the invitation was exciting, and Nustef wondered if Masiph had been elevated and was looking to fill out his quadra with some familiars.

"I'm sure he has a reason for inviting me today," he said, voicing his own thoughts.

"Yes, I'm sure he does."

He looked at her and she smiled. "I'm sorry. You know my heart aches without you."

"Yes. Whatever shall you do this afternoon to pass the dull hours?"

"Only my spinning."

"You need a spindle to spin," he said, taking her in his arms.

"I shall have to find a way to manage on my own till you return," she said, touching a finger to his lips.

"And what, my sweet woman, will you spin?"

"A badge, to replace the one that's abandoning me," she said, her hand straying lower.

He laughed. "Make it an arras. We can use it as if we were true Nohritais of worth."

"I will be waiting behind it when you return."

He embraced her again and then left for the long walk to Uenam district, thinking as he went of her distaste for the man. It was different for her, she had no name. The Ad Illied, though, were once a family of some repute, holding respectable positions in the state and the army. After the fall, one of his ancestors had even been a Vazeir of Delhen, but within three generations everything the family had was lost.

He had to pass the Pantheon of the Dead, the cemetery for many Nohritai families, to reach the part of Uenam where the Ad Ezern estate was, and though it was against his better judgment, he turned from his path. As a child his father had taken him weekly to see the Ad Illied mausoleum. All he could remember of it was the ruinous entrance overgrown with weeds. His father had described the shrine inside and the various tombs with candles that the Ceinobytes kept lit continuously. In his grandfather's time they had been unable to afford the payments for the candles and the Ceinobytes' blessings, and then they had been unable to pay the upkeep of the area around the tomb. The last indignity had come just before his own birth, when the Ceinobytes had locked the doors to the mausoleum and would not allow the family entrance.

He passed a group of supplicants on their way to some crypt as he walked along the Pantheon's main pathway, on their way, no doubt, to pay observance to some dead Nohritai they had adopted as a sage. He knew Liusir id Delluthen had a shrine here, and there were likely others as well. There were Ceinobytes as well, passing among the mausoleums to clean and ensure the candles were lit, or trimming the grass outside. Seeing them engaged in the tasks denied his own ancestors sent his pulse racing and he quickened his pace, the sooner to be done with this.

He nearly had to ask for directions—no greater humiliation could be imaginable—but after some wandering he found it, much as he remembered, the weeds and grass so overgrown that the mausoleum was nearly hidden. The entrance had mostly fallen away and the door itself looked as if it were only just clinging to its hinges. He noticed that the grass and weeds in front, though not cut, were trampled, which meant that some family was likely making their home there. Their souls were condemned to the lowest plain, though he doubted that concerned them greatly.

He resisted the urge to go inside and see what desecrations had been visited upon his ancestors. What further violation could there be than lying with his blasted plain-cursed grandfather and whatever indigents passed through? His father was condemned to a pauper's grave outside the city walls, unnamed, and in all likelihood condemned to pass eternity distant from his own kin. As was he.

It was difficult to think of his father—their days had not been easy together, and in their last years they had not spoken at all. Forced by the failures of his ancestors and the destitution of their estates to work as a common merchant in bird shops, his father had nursed his bitterness like he nursed his drink, quaffing both freely. He forbade his son to join him in his profession, insisting that he join the army, but Nustef was refused entry and had to join the Watch instead.

That had been the first of the disappointments he had sent his father's way. There had been more, but the final, the ultimate, had been Erise, a woman of no family, who worked as a seamstress. It was noble work by the standards of her ancestors, but he had wanted Nustef to marry into a Nohritai family, no matter how minor and impoverished, and begin the restoration of the family name.

Nustef had no regrets. He had a respectable life—Erise had to work, but many women suffered that fate—and now that he was a jetthir in the Watch they could save to open a shop of their own. They owed nothing to anyone, as Erise would say. Still, one's ancestors compelled, fathers especially. What hope did he have in the afterlife were he to disparage their spirits in this one?

Uenam was called the Walled City—and for good reason, as every estate, no matter its size, was surrounded by some type of barrier. The largest of them were almost palaces in their own right, with multiple gardens, their own private canals off the main waterways, and the family mausoleum housed on the grounds. The Ad Illied estate, a piddling thing by comparison, had once been on these streets, though it had been confiscated by the Vazeir with the rest of the Imperial grants and some great family had incorporated the building into its own grounds.

The streets were never as busy here, filled mostly with palanquins carried by porters, even more so after the raid with the Nohritai hardly daring to set foot in public. Where once some of the more daring Nohritai ladies would go about in open palanquins, seeing the world and having the world see them, now all the palanquins were covered and even the poorest had armed men escorting them. It seemed to Nustef that when he had been in the district previously, many of the gates to the estates had stood open with a guard at the entrance. Now they were closed and most of them had two men on watch. The atmosphere had been altered beyond recognition, both here and elsewhere. He felt like an intruder on better streets, with armed swords looking him over, though his wide sleeves and Craitolian silks marked him as a man of some worth.

In his own district there had been killings which had started a few days after the raid. The first had just been some whore, her face and body disfigured beyond recognition. The rest had been women as well, but of good repute, who worked as seamstresses or at food stands, or in the houses of merchants. They had all been murdered and marked in the same manner on their way to or from work. Erise worked in the house of a merchant near the army barracks, and anytime he was able to he would walk her there or meet her to bring her home. They were lucky in that the family would send someone to walk her home when he was unable. Still, fear permeated the most banal and everyday of activities.

The Ad Ezern estate was in the heart of Uenam. He was let in with hardly a glance, the men on watch familiar with him from his earlier visits during Masiph's recovery. One of them led him to the main house along a tree-shaded pathway. Behind the trees he caught glimpses of flowers and plants from parts unknown, flashes of water glinting in the sunlight. A eunuch greeted him at the door and led him through a series of well-appointed rooms to the aslyn chamber.

He always felt out of place here, a pathetic simulacrum of a Nohritai. In fact, he had never been in an aslyn room, though he recognized the accoutrements from his own reading of various chronicles. He had done all his chewing in public rooms or about his day. There was a low table which he sat at it, noting the rug on which he was seated, and which covered most of the small room, had woven into it scenes of what he assumed were the triumphs of the Ad Ezern.

Masiph entered and they embraced, exchanging the formal greetings, and then sat facing each other across the table. The eunuch returned carrying a tray, which he set in front of them. There was a bowl filled with belet leaves, a candle, an exquisite box which held the quid, and a spittoon. The eunuch set the candle and bowl on the table between them, lighting it while they each took a leaf from the bowl. They blessed their ancestors and spoke an invocation to the highest plain and then burned the leaves. The blessing done, the eunuch removed the lid to the box with a flourish, revealing the aslyn quid lying within, and retreated from the room with a bow.

After a bit of sucking and chewing to get the aslyn started, Nustef broke their silence. "The city has gone mad. There was not a woman about today in Uenam."

Masiph smiled. "I know. Even Nes Masis is staying covered these days."

"Perhaps her palanquin is full."

"She is an accommodating woman."

"You've been keeping yourself busy." He tried to keep his tone light.

"Busier lately." Masiph adjusted the quid in his mouth and let out a stream of orange saliva into the spittoon at their feet. "I'm sorry it's been so long. Quite honestly, I didn't take the whole coronation well."

"I wondered."

"I struggled with it. Felt like I'd been put to the squeak, you know."

"Still," Nustef said. "Such an honor to get an audience with Ad Eselte."

"Yes. Yes. But there was no pleasure in it. I felt like a newly cracked maiden, thinking of nothing but the spoiling done to me."

He shrugged, as though it had just been a fleeting mood and all was in the past. "I think they only did it to get me out of the Watch. In case there is another attack. I don't know why; it's clear Ibrazol has already decided I'm not fit to head the family. No mention of my marriage, no talk of elevation."

Nustef nodded in sympathy. "It's only a matter of time, though. They can't coronate you without elevating you eventually."

Masiph shrugged to say that they very well could do that.

The aslyn was beginning to take effect. Nustef's cheek was tingling and there was the tiny burst of euphoria that reached through his head. He spat, "Even your father, though, would have to admit that you were deserving of honor. What you did, going into that house, not knowing what was in there, to save that family is incredible."

"I didn't save them, though."

"The thought not the deed, or whatever the sages say. Anyway, you did far more than any of us on the wall that night."

Masiph looked away. "Anything new on the wall? I'm sure Achelluth sends his regards."

Nustef laughed. "Yes, I'll be sure and tell him you send yours. I think he misses you. He could not lose to you at dice. Other than that."

"Well, you are jetthir now, though. I had forgotten, speaking of honors. A most deserving one."

Nustef nodded in thanks. "The coin is appreciated. It's the same old tedium, though. All quiet, day or night."

Their conversation led them to the peculiar madness that seemed to have taken hold in the capital, as though the same malady had struck untold thousands and they were now overwhelmed by the same feverish dreams of ransacking Shadow Men, though there had been no sightings of the Shadows since the raid. Nustef spoke of the murders in his district and Masiph spoke of some others in one of the drinkery roads just outside Uenam, where the Nohritai youth were known to frequent. Of course, the Shadows were blamed for all these desecrations.

"I heard a conspiracy just the other day about your father," Nustef said. "One of the men on the wall. He told me that the Shadows could pass as Renians because of some alkemyc concoction, and they had killed your father and replaced him at the Ad Eselte's side."

"I hadn't heard that, though it does have the ring of truth to it. I've heard that some of the Great Families are in league with the Shadows and helped organize the raid as a pretext to make the Ad Eselte look weak so they could manufacture his overthrow."

"I guess people have to pass their days some way. Though I'm surprised the Palace hasn't done more, given all the talk you keep hearing."

"I was in to see my father the other day," Masiph said. "When I left my audience there was a jetthir of the army waiting. Which is strange, because Ibrazol has no jurisdiction over the army."

"What do you think he was there for?"

"I don't know. But maybe they are preparing something."

Nustef considered this for a moment. "Not an invasion."

"Into the desert? Hardly. Maybe an attack, if they can figure where the Shadows are at."

"Strange."

"Yes." He shrugged. "If I am elevated, and I honestly don't know if it will happen, but if I am, I would like you to join my cohort. I could arrange it, I think."

"Yes," Nustef said immediately. "I would be forever in your debt."

He spat and smiled as the spittoon rang.

# 28

"Bugger won't stay down."

Hieran awoke to those words echoing around his head, unsure where they had emerged from. He tried opening his eyes and succeeded, only to be faced with another shade of darkness. After a time he was able to distinguish the shadow from substance and recognize the cell where he had been attacked. Those words, he recalled, had been spoken by one of the hired arms right before the final blows descended.

He tried to sit up and managed that as well, though he nearly vomited as his equilibrium vibrated like a guitar string. While he gathered himself—it felt like his head had swelled beyond the stretching point of his skin—he took a measure of the cell. The door, which he was facing, was wood, with a bit of grating at eye level to allow someone to peer in or out. He decided he was not up to that just yet. The cell itself was small, perhaps less than three paces along each wall. How had the three of them fit in here? Perhaps only one of them had beat on him. His memory was scattered there and on the moments before.

He did remember something of the estate and of his walk from the barracks. He collected an image of that as best he could, and along with what he visualized of the cell, he passed it to Tehh. There was no response, though he waited in expectation for a good while after his breathing had returned to normal from the effort he had expended.

Gods curse the old fool, he thought, and slammed his fist

against the stone of the wall. It wasn't as though he hadn't received the message. Now that they had been bound, Disciple to Adept, they shared this link as well, and Tehh could no more refuse the images of his Disciple than he could close his door to the Gver.

In the early days of the Council, when the binding of practitioners of the art had just begun, the Adepts only beginning to realize the power granted by the balance of two in forming alkemy, some of those bound went mad from the images passing back and forth between them. It was, Hieran knew from experience, a terrifying moment whenever these images would just appear unnanounced in the mind, a thought truly unbidden. And, for what reasons no one knew, only the image itself came—the rest of the thought and feeling and soul of the person was left behind, leaving only a moment frozen from the ether of the mind.

A fury seized him, barely contained. What was the old fool doing? He wanted, so desperately wanted, to let go that discipline, instilled in him from his first moments as an initiate in the Council, and unleash whatever foul and unspeakable images lay in his mind, let them pass through that link which led from his mind to Tehh's. Let them pass, let them gnaw at his brain till he was paralyzed and slobbering and broken. Of course he wouldn't. To do so would mean his death. Council law was very clear on these matters and others: alkemya could not be directed upon those who did not practice it, except in the most extreme instances, nor could the astral of any such person be drawn upon to shape the germ of alkemy. To do so was known as scouring, and it left the victim without normal mental and spiritual faculties, if they survived. These were the laws they lived by.

As his anger subsided somewhat, he became aware that his clothes were soaked through. For a terrifying moment he thought it might somehow be blood, but then he noticed the steady patter of rain that had apparently been present all along. Turning, he saw a grate above him, wide enough for him to slip a fist through, and outside what appeared to be dusk settling. The stones on which he had been lying were damp to the touch, and in places there were pools of water.

How had he not noticed that before? Just a blow to the head, he told himself, but he was starting to become concerned. He thought about sending to Tehh again, deciding against it. There was nothing for it, the bastard would act on his own time.

What he did decide to do was get up and away from the water. He had just gotten to his feet, still feeling his way through his unsteadiness, when the cell door was flung open. A gentleman, clearly a noble of rank, walked in, a look of distaste plain on his face. Behind him stood the two hired swords, hands near their weapons, glaring in at Hieran. He recognized the noble as the Chair of Morning, a frivolous man by reputation. The fleshiness of his face and gut suggested a devotion to pleasure, though the hardness of his expression just now belied that. Sedar, the name came to him.

"I am on business from the Palace," he said.

"I know," Sedar said, unperturbed. Shadow and light flickered along his face as the lamp in the cellar outside sputtered.

"They know I am here."

"You've told the old man, have you?" A hint of a smile. "Are you certain he'll be able to remember where?"

Hieran frowned but did not respond and Sedar's smile grew, though there was little mirth in it. "The Gver has no right or call to be sending agents, especially an Adept's underling to Morning property."

*So this is the song we'll play.* Aloud, he said, "I am here officially. I made no secret to anyone I spoke to of why I was here."

"Are you now a Magister, in addition to your being an alkemycal lackey?"

When the Disciple did not reply, Sedar gave a snort of disgust. "I thought not. There are laws in place and the Gver and his minions are required to observe as well as enforce them. Best that you and he and the rest keep that in mind. If his Most Glorious wishes to investigate the disappearance of some third-rank defender, he can feel free to send a Magister, in full uniform, who will announce himself at our gates. Any of us then will answer any questions he might have."

"I am actually here with regards to a Fennen, formerly a palace guard. He was found gutted in the alley behind one of your taverns."

If he had hoped to see some sort of reaction from this revelation, he was disappointed. Sedar did not so much as blink.

"Be that as it may," the Chair of the Morning said, "send a Magister. Officially. And my people will answer any questions put to them."

Of course, anyone who might potentially know something that would incriminate the Morning would be mysteriously absent once the Magistery made it through the gates, much to the chagrin of his hosts.

"You, my young friend, though," Sedar continued, "are trespassing and guilty of espionage. You have no right here and you know it."

"You have no right to imprison me. You can evict me from this property, but that is all."

"You are not a noble of the rank."

"True," Hieran said, surprising himself with his aggrieved tone. "But I do have the seal of the Gver."

Sedar's vicious smile, poison come for dinner, returned. "The Gver cannot operate with impunity, whatever he might believe. You would think that recent events might have suggested as much to him."

And there the song did change, Hieran thought with some surprise. He did not bother with a reply and Sedar left, his mercenaries closing the cell door and bolting it shut with a violent ringing of iron. He turned and walked gingerly around his meager space, trying to find a spot that was at least somewhat untouched by the rainwater. Failing that, he sat down, shivering a bit at the cold and the damp, and tried to pass the time till dawn.

The next morning, not long after first light, a young Magister arrived at the Morning gates investigating Hieran's disappearance. He was not refused entry, he could not be, and was led to the Chair of the Morning's estate. They were waiting for him in the hall just beyond the entryway: the Chair of Morning, some functionary, two swordsmen, and a disheveled and exhausted Hieran.

Before the Magister had a chance to ask about this clear violation of law, Sedar stepped forward and announced that he wished to lodge a formal complaint against the Gver for the violation of the rights of the Morning.

The Magister opened his mouth to respond, but at a shake of the head from Hieran simply nodded and said that he would have an adjunct sent over to draw up the complaint and that the Magistery would investigate.

Sedar thanked him graciously for attending to the matter and then excused himself, saying there were pressing matters he needed to attend to. The Magister watched, somewhat amazed, as everyone left the room but Hieran and the attendant who had brought him to the house. He opened his mouth again, unsure exactly how to proceed.

"This way, gentlemen," the attendant said smoothly into the void, and led the three of them back outside. A light drizzle had started.

When they were safely outside the gates and past the Morning grounds, the Magister turned to Hieran and asked, cautiously, "Would you also like to file a complaint?"

The Disciple looked at him as though he were an astounding idiot. A gush of relief went through the Magister's body. It had been plain to him that this matter was well beyond his rank and now he knew how to proceed. The adjunct would be sent to take down the Chair's complaint, but nothing would be done by the Magistery and the doing of things would return to the realm of the shadows.

"Did they not send you with a damn palanquin?" the Disciple said, looking up into the rain in exasperation.

# 29

The clouds were massing above as Masiph strolled down Emerald Row, his silks damp and oppressive in the humid air. The street was bright with color from the awnings of the jewel shops that were scattered along its path. He dodged among the fruit vendors and various hawkers, ignoring their entreaties, keeping his hand on his purse as he did so. Emerald Row was as notorious for its pickpockets as it was for its jewelers, thieves of a different sort. He was not here looking for baubles for a mistress or a gullible lover, however. Nazeed had dispatched him to deliver a message. He kept his pace at a saunter, careful not to move down the road too fast. The person was supposed to contact him and he wanted to make sure he was not missed.

His heartbeat quickened as he came to main part of the Row, where the jewel shops were clustered together. He felt exposed as he was enveloped in the swell of the crowd that always formed around the shops, a mishmash lot from all avenues of life, and he fingered the dagger he had hidden along with his purse within the folds of his robes. If they or anyone wanted to kill him, he reminded himself, they had ample opportunity almost any day that he set foot on the street.

Nazeed had given him this day's instructions the night before last at a rundown brothel, where a few of their conspirators had joined them for some surreptitious cups. Masiph had been excited about the additional members at their meeting, which he took as a sign of Nazeed's growing trust. Lisser was not present, though the boy Jheupp was and he latched onto Masiph, recounting in excruciating detail his grievances against the Ad Eselte and his disgust for the impurity of their days. The others names he did not get, and he wondered if they recognized him, though it was doubtful they would.

Their usual gatherings were over quickly, barely long enough for Masiph to get his instructions. Here, though, they idled for over an hour, the hostess and the girls leaving them be. Eventually Nazeed excused himself and went upstairs with a girl. The rest of them glanced at each other but stayed where they were, continuing to whisper amongst themselves and eye anyone who walked through the door.

Growing impatient, Masiph excused himself and went to the back to relieve himself. The pots were under another set of stairs above, and when he was finished with his business he, flushed with his cups, decided to go up. He was almost at the top of the stairs when he heard Nazeed's voice and froze. Someone replied with an accent Masiph couldn't hear well enough to place. Realizing that they were saying their farewells, he returned to the bottom of the stairs and waited, fidgeting by the chamber closet as though it were full and watched as the foreigner came down the stairs and went out into the alley. By his robes he was from Luessan.

When he returned to the table, Nazeed was already back and they were preparing to leave. He looked Masiph over, his eyes still and hard, his face betraying nothing. Masiph could only hope that his was the same. As they had started on their separate ways on the street, Nazeed had pulled him aside and Masiph had been certain that his spying had been found out. Nazeed made no mention of it though, simply giving him his instructions for today.

The whole thing had felt wrong to him then and still did. Did Nazeed suspect he had seen him in league with the Luessan? And what sort of conspiracy were they involved in that included Luessans? Masiph's doubts about the entire enterprise had been growing by the day, fed mostly by his dissatisfaction at being kept ignorant of their greater purpose, of which he had been given only the vaguest of details beyond what Osiphan had told him that first night. If he was to risk his life and the honor of the Ad Ezern, he wanted to be more than a mere errand boy. With each day the danger grew further, for now they were in league with enemies of the empire. To what end?

He had spent most of the night before awake worrying at these thoughts, telling himself that he shouldn't come today. It felt wrong. Nothing good could come of it. But he needed to know what would happen. He needed to know. There was no reason to any of this, he thought.

An unseen hand seized his shoulder. "Young man, unlucky in love? I have some elixirs that will seize the heart of any woman you desire."

Masiph turned, feeling his stomach tumble away as he did. Looking at the "hawker," he almost laughed. He was dressed as a street healer selling his magic elixirs, with the white cap and the shabby robe. His hands were clean, though, and his hair well kept, so it was clear to anyone who bothered to look closely that he was of better provenance.

"I might be interested in something for a sore tooth," he replied.

"Of course, of course. I have just the thing." He pulled a thin vial filled with an ugly yellow liquid from his robes and waved it in Masiph's face.

"It looks like piss," Masiph said, taking the vial and holding it up to the light.

"Quite, quite. It is the urine of a lyseth, quite rare. Warm it a bit, and a squeeze of limon for taste and it will clarify your tooth, among other things. Just the thing. Two kenir."

Masiph tried to look unconvinced. "Piss for a toothache."

"Oh yes. Naussien id Healler noted that the urine of the lyseth worked wonders for both toothaches and arthritis. If you mix it with my guaranteed life elixir, the concoction will excite your spirit and dry even the sodden."

"What is in that?"

"A family recipe, I'm afraid. Guaranteed, of course. I can assure you of its quality."

"Everything is pure, nothing is pure."

"Quite, quite. Three kenir for both," the healer said, nodding vigorously again.

Masiph paid the man and took the vials. He stopped and inquired after the price of some emeralds for a necklace at a jeweler's before heading back for Uenam.

# 30

The usual torpor that seized the vessel and its inhabitants following midday was shattered by the arrival of a new passenger. Vyissan did not know the name of the town—it seemed to him a sleepy sort of place of little note—but the new arrival was nothing of the sort, striding aboard with a regal bearing. Four slaves and an attendant followed in his wake, by far the largest retinue of anyone on board, one that was certain to complicate the arrangements on the smaller ship that followed in their wake.

Vyissan watched as one of the second officers approached the man and was rebuffed with an imperious wave and a loud declaration that he would speak only to the captain of the vessel. The second officer led him below deck, where the captain had sequestered himself. What followed was a heated conversation between the two men, most of which Vyissan had little trouble hearing above deck, ending with the captain agreeing to give over his quarters for the duration of their journey. Later he discovered that the man was a relation of the Ad Feina, which apparently commanded respect in the Empire, but at the time he was simply left amazed at the proceedings.

The next day the new arrival joined the group of men who gathered every afternoon they were not at dock on the aft deck for a game of cards in the shade of an awning. Vyissan would sometimes wander over to watch the matches, if only to gain a bit of shelter from the afternoon heat. He never played, though some of the games were familiar to him. The Renians had a different ranking of cards, with the Gver being highest, followed by the Qraul, and he did not want to chance that he would forget that in the heat of a hand and betray his origins. The stakes in some of the games were often higher than he was comfortable with, and he was not alone in that. There were usually more watching than playing, and that was particularly the case once the Ad Feina joined the table.

One of the men who left the play when the Ad Feina drove the betting high joined him on the side, swearing under his breath and staring hard at the new arrival. He spat, though the other did not notice as he was busy making a show of his slave bringing a bottle of wine from his own personal collection for him to drink.

"What is his name?" Vyissan asked.

"Nassen id Uthelar."

"He is of the Ad Feina, I've heard."

"Married into them, yes. The Ad Uthelar are not so illustrious, but if you are unlucky enough to speak with him you will find out that the cousin of his wife is Uselen id Feina."

"I'm sorry," Vyissan said. "The name is familiar but I can't place it."

"It's said his brother has the ear of the Emperor."

"An important family, no doubt. Strange that he would find himself on this ship."

"Are you watching him?" the other snorted. "This is exactly the ship he was looking for."

"Nohritai always have the money," someone else said to them under his breath.

The man beside him nodded violently while Vyissan shrugged and they all turned to watch the game. Most of the others had folded their hands and there were now only two players, the Nohritai Nassen and Gethuul. The man had contrived to place himself in Vyissan's sightline each time they left the vessel, and at every stop at port staring with a discomforting intensity. Vyissan briefly considered abandoning the vessel and finding a new ship to Darrhyn, but if he were in fact an Imperial agent then doing so would only serve to confirm whatever suspicions he had.

Gethuul was not doing well here, though, already down badly against the Ad Feina and responding by betting even higher for each trick while Nassen taunted him. In two more hands he had exhausted his funds and was left wincing at the mound of coins opposing him. Watching this display, Vyissan knew he was not an Imperial agent—no authority would willingly draw so much attention. Just a fool then, though the thought did little to relieve him.

"You don't belong in this game. I've known eunuchs with more ability," Nassen declared. Gethuul flushed and drained his cup, still staring at the pile of coins. "Why don't you leave the table? Perhaps someone with some real coin and a spirited root to stand on can step up here."

Gethuul set his cup down and slowly got out of his seat, walking away. Nassen watched him go and then turned to those standing around. "Well. No one? If I had known I was coming aboard such an unseminared ship I might have thought twice about it."

No one among those around the table replied, all of them refusing to meet the Nohritai's eyes. He smirked and was about to say something when Gethuul returned and flung some papers on the table.

"This is the stake in my house. We have interests in assenta flowers that will be worth five hundred kenir at least in the next two months if they can be gotten back down to Sylaron in that time. I'll wager that against you. Do you have the purse and the stones to match it?"

"Of course," Nassen said. A hush gripped the rest of those assembled. Five hundred kenir was no jousting sum. The two played out the hand in silence, only the gargle of the current intruding, along with the oar strokes of the slaves. Vyissan closed his eyes and let the sound wash over him. There were birds singing as well in trees along the shore, and laughter from the boat following them. He opened his eyes to see the hand going badly for Gethuul and stepped away from the table to continue his reverie. Outside the awning the heat was oppressive and the clouds were gathering above for the afternoon rains. Trees crowded the shoreline on both sides of the river, an impenetrable mass of foliage and shadow.

# 31

Donier idled in the courtyard where the Aghuerl servant had brought him. He was at the center of a garden of citrus trees, which obscured the estate house and the walls that surrounded him. The smell of lime and lemon was heavy on the air. Ludenn arrived from the main house, offering greetings and clapping him on the shoulder to lead him deeper into the garden to a marble fountain. At a gesture from Ludenn they sat on its lip, Donier running his hand through the water beside them.

"What brings you, my friend?" Ludenn said.

"Thank you for taking the time." Ludenn waved him away. "I have a favor to ask. If it is too great, then please let me know."

As he spoke, the servant who had brought him to the courtyard materialized from the trees around them with a bottle of wine and two cups on a tray. He poured them each a measure and then left. They toasted each others health and then Ludenn motioned from his second to continue.

"It is about Terainous." Ludenn nodded gravely. "It is not my place to intervene, but I cannot help myself. I was to see his wife some days ago."

"Liene."

"Yes. She is having a trying time. The family will not accept our verdict that Terainous has passed to the hall. They will not release her dowry and she cannot return to her own family and she cannot mourn."

"There are other sons, are there not?" Ludenn said, and Donier nodded and gestured with his hand the rolling of coins through his fingers.

Ludenn shook his head. "Troublesome indeed. There is little the cohort can do beyond what we have already done."

"I know. She was hoping...she asked if we might approach the Gver to intercede on her behalf. Perhaps authorize another search...or something that might give further proof that Terainous has gone from this realm."

Ludenn considered this. "That man will do nothing unless she prays before him. She does have a fine mouth for invocations. Coin will need to be stamped for this, no doubt. Maybe it's you who prefers to put your head upon it."

Donier did not reply, and both of them sipped at their wine, Ludenn grinning. "Best to put this from your mind. There is nothing for you to do. Hurt enough in our lives to take on that of others."

They left it at that, finishing their wine and talking of the business of the cohort. The Shadows had begun the raiding season in earnest, slipping past the pyrsedies and into the eastern estates, and as a result all the Gver's cohorts were required to patrol the highways east of Lastl. They were due to go out in the next week, and Ludenn had yet to name a second to replace Terainous.

On his way back to the Afieled estate, Donier was hailed by Uherl a Deyra, a noble of the third rank and an old friend. In their youths, before his marriage and his induction into the cohort, they had passed many an afternoon together in wastrel times, as they were known, drinking and pining after maids they could not have, fighting and dueling at the slightest provocation, and cursing the fate and poor rank of birth that had left them without a part in the Realm.

Their paths had diverged after Donier had become a second and secured a favorable marriage, and he had seen little of Uherl in the last five years. Seeing him now reminded him of the fine times, the bitterness and squabbling forgotten, and was a fine glass of wine after the bitter ale of his talk with Ludenn. Uherl insisted on a bottle, and Donier, not wanting to find an excuse, agreed, and they found their way to the nearest drinkery.

After the news of the last five years had been exhausted, along with most of the bottle, Uherl said to him, "You seem happy. The years have been kind."

"Yes. And you as well."

Uherl waved his hand. "I try. There is much that is ill in the Realm."

"Always."

"The trunk is strong, but the roots are sodden."

"Like our Gver."

"Yes, yes," Uherl laughed. "Nothing has changed there. We are condemned to the reign of the impure."

He poured them both a final measure from the bottle. "I wonder, do you still think on our days with the Golden Veil?"

Donier shrugged and held open his hands. "I left them a long time ago."

"Yes, we both felt the wind changing direction," Uherl said, and then began to talk about his wife's family.

Donier nodded as his friend spoke, only partially listening to what he said, his mind still on the name Uherl had uttered. The Golden Veil. A name that had once struck terror in the hearts of the Great Families of Craitol. It had begun in Takyl, a gang of young nobleman of low rank, second sons and the like, who had banded together during their wastrel years. There were similar gangs throughout all the cities of the Realm, young men with nothing better to do, but most spent their time in settling feuds with each other, or setting upon the unsuspecting of the plebeian classes for sport. Most of them were organized around one of the factions, betting on the matches and the like.

The Golden Veil had been much the same, tied to the Morning and feuding with the Evening, but their dissatisfaction with Gver Duirhe a Takyl, who had excluded most of their families from positions in court or cohort, grew so profound that they began to attack those in the Great Families. The Herald and Gatekeeper of the city were both murdered in the bed they had been sharing in the Atakyl Palace, their faces marked with the sign of blasphemy. It was not long before such actions spread to other cities in the Realm, the various gangs of excluded finding common cause, joined in some cases by the conjurers in the Council of Adepts who had been excluded from the upper ranks.

A reign of terror was briefly ignited, any number of important men were killed and even a few women, until the Gvers and their cohorts struck back, storming the estate homes of those they knew were part of the Veil and arresting they and their families. Property was seized, fathers imprisoned, and sons executed, and as quickly as it had risen the Veil dissolved.

Donier and Uherl had both been a part of the Veil in Lastl, though only at its fringes and only for a time. Neither had been trusted enough to undertake anything of significance, and neither had had the strength of conviction to act on their own, as some others did. That had saved them in the end, for by the time the crackdown had begun both had been more or less excised. In Donier's case, he had left following his induction into the cohort and had carried out some of the raids against his former comrades.

All of that was in the not-so-distant past now. Donier had not been a part of the Veil for almost seven years and the group's name had not been heard in nearly five, so utterly had they been crushed. Which was why it was strange of Uherl to bring it up, especially since it was a time in their past, his especially, that was difficult to explain easily. He understood why later once the wine was done and they were both readying to go.

"You have been a second five years now?" Uherl said to him as they exited the drinkery to the sunshine of the day. "You were always one to work hard," he added after Donier nodded. "You should have a cohort by now."

"I do not have the family for it."

"No, not now or ever, unless a new dawn should rise." Uherl glanced sideways at him as they walked down the street, Donier staying quiet and keeping his face still, and then seized him by the elbow, drawing him in close. The street was quiet but not empty and they were near no doors or shops, Donier noted.

"You know what happened in the Palace. That was the first step, the first light on the horizon," Uherl said, his mouth so close to Donier's ear he could almost feel his tongue moving to sound the words. "There will be more to follow."

They both waited as someone brushed past them. Uherl did not speak again until he was well out of earshot. "There is a place for you if you want it. Your position would be useful."

Donier smiled. "I will think on it."

Uherl held his eyes for a long moment, trying to pierce the veil. "Good, good. Think on it. We will talk again. So good that I chanced upon you."

They parted ways and Donier made his way home, taking a circuitous route to see if he was being followed. There had been nothing to chance about that meeting, he now knew. No doubt he would be seeing Uherl again, and next time he might not ask for his service—it might be demanded. If they had been involved in the attack on the Gver, rumors of which had been swirling for days, then it was not a small game they were playing. They intended a revolution and they would use the leverage Uherl had on him in whatever manner gave them greatest advantage.

The wine had turned in Donier's stomach by the time he reached home, and he ate little for dinner, retiring to his quarters early. His dreams, when he at last found his way to sleep, were of the desert again, as they had been on many nights since the Feast of Balance. The valley was the same, every time, as were the endless steps he took and the horizon he could glimpse at far end of his vision.

# 32

The sun was not yet visible in the sky, though a dim sort of light pervaded the streets of Darrhyn. The only people about at this hour were bakers or people bringing their goods to market from outside the city. In spite of the growing light, Masiph stumbled into Lisser, eliciting a string of whispered curses from the man. He thought better of apologizing and instead sought to rub the sleep from his eyes. Already he had managed to be late in arriving at their meeting spot, and now he was tripping over his partner. He glanced over at him, trying to gauge how serious an offense he had just committed, but he could discern nothing from the man's stony countenance.

He decided he was too tired to care, and certainly it seemed he was too exhausted to think anything through to its end. For days after he had delivered his message to the man on Emerald Row Masiph had heard nothing from Nazeed or Lisser. There had been no meetings, no tasks assigned him. It was as though he had been forgotten. For a time he had wondered if he had failed some test, or if they had grown suspicious of him, sensing his doubts. It had been a relief in so many ways, and he had almost allowed himself to believe that they had cast him aside. Instead, Nazeed had found him the day before and told him when and where he was to meet Lisser. No further explanation had been given and Masiph had spent a sleepless night, trying to convince himself not to go, certain that they were about to murder him for his faithlessness in their cause, only at the very last minute to find himself rushing to get to the appointed spot where Lisser awaited him.

What their purpose was Masiph could not say, but he felt safe enough. If they had intended to murder him, it would have been done by now. They were in a nondescript neighborhood, the sort of place one would pass through by day without comment, but which, emptied of people and in the dim red light of morning, seemed strange to Masiph. The streets were lined with haphazard multi-storied buildings, some with walls, all surrounding courtyards, of the sort that could be found on any street in the Empire. Many of these would have quarters that let by the month, the sort of places where merchants or travelers passing through the city might make their home. Lisser spotted some landmark on the street and led them into the alleys. Masiph could see him counting the buildings as they walked past.

When he reached his count, Lisser looked about the alley and then, satisfied that they were alone, picked at the lock to the servants' door of the building. It only took a moment and they were in, Lisser raising a warning finger to his lips before proceeding to the stairs and the second floor. This was a later addition, both the stairs and the second story, judging by the different coloring of the brick and stone above and below. As with so many of these places, the rooms had once been individual homes built by squatters that had been joined together and built upon as the neighborhood grew in wealth and respect. They skirted along the wall, trying to stay in the shadows and out of sight of the courtyard below, though it was empty, a grave stillness suspended throughout. Masiph counted three doors before Lisser came to a stop.

The door was already unlocked and they went in, passing through the main room and its scant furniture to the bedroom. A stunningly beautiful woman, a quid of aslyn in her cheek, sat at the foot of the bed, one leg crossed over the other. On the bed, amidst a tangle of sheets, lay a man, naked, his penis still firmly erect. He was dead, Masiph knew instantly, looking him over. Far too rigid, he thought, and then had to stop himself from laughing.

As if he had read his mind, Lisser frowned at him and then turned to the woman. "You are not supposed to be here."

"I know." Lisser had whispered but she spoke in a normal voice, rich with an undercurrent of laughter. Masiph found himself entranced by her eyes, the irises almost as dark as the pupils, which were almost as dark as the hair that tumbled about her shoulders.

"Why?" Lisser whispered, his anger apparent.

"Had I known he was as tight with coin as he was with his ass, I might not have considered. I will remind you that I was promised whatever spoils were here."

"You've left your spoil on the bed."

She glanced at the body behind her with a smile. "That fruit smells off, and my appetite remains."

"You truly are a cannibal. I don't know what you expect of me, though. That was the risk you took."

"No," she said, her voice louder, ignoring an urgent stare from Lisser. "I was promised treasure in exchange for unlocking mine, and I mean to have it."

Lisser stared at her, his face flushed. She returned his gaze, her eyes daring him to contradict her. Masiph noticed her toes were painted scarlet, as were her lips, matching the outer robe she wore, so loose that it looked as though it would slide off her shoulders with ease.

"It seems he did not have time to unlock the treasury," Lisser hissed at her, pulling his coin purse out from within his robes and tossing it at her. "That will have to be enough."

She caught it easily and then tested the weight in her hand. "Kenir?" she asked, and received a nod from Lisser.

She nodded in return. "He did not have the coin to pay the customs necessary for this wholesale."

She stood as she said it, and for the first time glanced at Masiph, who was still hopelessly lost in her beauty. Her lips curled slightly, somehow both inviting and menacing, and then she flicked her eyes over to the bed where the corpse lay. He followed her gaze and felt his own penis stiffen even as his mouth went dry. Her smile broadened, as if she knew what was happening, and she walked past, almost brushing against him, leaving him swimming in her scent of wildflower and aslyn.

Lisser was staring at him with a disdainful grin on his face. "Careful," he said. "They say she likes to collect them." He gestured toward the bed.

Masiph walked over and studied the dead man. He had a startled look to his face that might have been funny in another circumstance.

"How does she do it?" he asked.

"Poison," Lisser said. "Some concoction of her own from the gen frog. She is both the vulture and the carrion."

Masiph nodded. Women of a lower element unhappy with their husbands had been known to add a gen frog to the pot to rid themselves of that nuisance.

"Never mind that," Lisser said. "Help me look through his papers."

He sent Masiph back to the main room, telling him to look for maps. There was a desk that the woman had broken into, throwing papers everywhere in her quest for valuables. He picked through everything on the floor and then started through the drawers. Most of what he saw were contracts, receipts, and the like. The man was a Factor for a Luessan company, a minor trader by the look of the letters, hardly worth the expense of having him killed by the likes of that woman.

The maps were in one of the drawers and he studied them before calling Lisser. They provided an answer of sorts to the assassination, though he wasn't sure what exactly. They were surveys of the northern border region where Renuih and Luessan gave way to a tribal region, covered in valuable forest that both sides claimed but neither could control. He had no idea what this meant. Obviously this was related to the Luessan man who had met with Nazeed, though how he could not say.

He called Lisser into the room, handing the maps over to him. Lisser thumbed through them before rolling them up, and then, without a word, he turned and left the quarters, leaving Masiph to scramble after him. When they were out on the streets, now starting to get busier, he almost had to run to keep up. All the while he thought about what this had been about. Were they in league with the Luessans or trying to thwart them? He couldn't say. And how did all this fit with an insurrection against the Ad Eselte, for that was what this was all supposed to be about wasn't it? All he knew for certain was that he was now tied to a murder, and that by the time he knew anything about this conspiracy it would be too late for him to make any sort of decision about which side he would be best to find himself on.

# 33

The storehouse was squat and ugly, most of its windows dark from filth that no one bothered to scrub away. A faint air of decay hung about it, the result of the beginnings of an unseen entropy working its rot on the complex. The entrance, though, was bright with new wood and paint, an inviting doorway and inside, Hieran knew firsthand, was a welcoming storefront. What lay beyond the office in the warehouse was obscured by the grimy windows.

He was not interested in what the warehouse held, though he suspected it was mostly empty given the paucity of traffic he had observed passing in and out of the storefront. No law in trade but customs, as the saying went. And customs could be circumvented too. In truth he was not certain what he was looking for, or who, for that was what it came to in the end. He was hoping for something to appear, though that would tell him one way or the other the involvement of the Currlene merchant house in the conspiracy against the Gver. His preference was for it to happen soon. The waiting was beginning to wear on him.

Amusingly, to himself at least, he was dressed as a penitent Cureder calling on passersby to join the faithful. There was a Melinist cloister nearby, one that emphasized her inhabitation of the three realms: the earthly, the heavens, and the underworld. If he had it correctly, and he very well might not, this sect taught that just as Melinon inhabited the three realms simultaneously so could each person, provided they could achieve the correct state of being. "Receptiveness to the moment" was how they put it. Achieving receptiveness involved much chanting and singing, and judicious use of mythres or duistel, or, if one believed some of the more interesting rumors, sex.

He had spent most of yesterday lurking in a tavern which offered a decent view of the storefront from down the street. Going there again, he had decided yesterday, might attract too much attention, so he had struck on his current disguise, which would allow him to move about the street without drawing much notice. He had a feeling that he would find himself in the tavern before the day was done, for it promised to be unbearably hot. Unless he somehow got lucky and this seemingly interminable watch led to something of import, but he did not hold out much hope for that.

It was Lazul's woman who had led him here. One of the other agents Tehh had put on the investigation had discovered her existence the day of Hieran's release from the Morning prison. She was a dancer with the Morning and the agent had managed to find out where she was entertaining that evening. How the man had done this without ending up in the Morning prison infuriated Hieran only slightly less than knowing that he was the one who had to spend the evening outside some third-rank nobleman's estate waiting for her.

She was very young, perhaps no more than fifteen, but with that aged look about the eyes already that suggested the hardness that was to come when her beauty had been crystallized by the life's various hardships. He waited until she and the two girls with her had been escorted back to their shared quarters just off the Morning grounds by the hired sword. When the man had gone he approached their door and kocked upon it. He heard some whispers and then footsteps as one of them approached the door. It opened and he found himself face to face with a dagger held by Lazul's woman.

"We have no coins on us," she told him, staring at the hands he held out to signal he was unarmed.

"I doubt that," he replied. "Perhaps you'd care to make some?"

From within the room one of her companions said,. "You don't have the stamp for our bargain."

"Oh, I have firm metal as necessary."

"Likely, they all say that after they've had their cups."

"We have the treasure you'd care to mine," she said, gesturing with her dagger. "Your tiny bauble does not have the worth of this."

He smiled at her. "It has a noble rank, though it may not look it. But my interests lie elsewhere. This would involve answering some questions."

"All of us?" one of her companions said.

"Just you," he said, pointing at the girl, still smiling.

She eyed him suspiciously, but he could tell he had intrigued her. His smile deepened. "Come to see me tomorrow. I'll be at the Tierien all day. We can talk then."

"How much coin?" she said.

"Enough," he told her. "The Tierien. I'll buy you a meal."

She came of course: who turned down a meal and the offer of coin? He ordered the food and an ale for her and let her finish it before he started questioning her. She had been Lazul's woman for a little more than half a year. It had not been widely known, for the Morning, as with the other factions, preferred their dancers not take up with third-rank stringers with no prospects. She did not know where he was. All he had told her before disappearing was that he had a job with the Currlene House and would be gone some time. She hadn't believed him, or at least she had assumed that he would not ever be coming back. His failure to return had not aroused any suspicion nor any bitterness, events had gone as life to that point had taught her they would.

The Currlene did much of their business for the Apysel, the bitter rival to the Alastl, so their involvement in hiring the man who tied up the assassination attempt's loose ends implied that the conspiracy was not local in scale. The utter indifference Nes Sedar put on display in imprisoning Hieran was made much less brazen if the Apysel were involved. It was said that Gver Pevertle favoured the Morning. Many things were said about Gver Pervelte—none of them particularly comforting for those who might displease him.

Hieran had not been the least surprised to discover the Apysel implicated in a plot against the Alastl, even the Gver himself, for the two families were always at war in the realm of shadows. One needed look no further than the killings this past winter for an example. The use of one of Kercubegahedd's agents, current or former, was of greater concern. All the Great Families had foresworn the false alkemya to this point. Maybe the High Adept had been a target as well, although they would have had no way of knowing that his Disciple would not be there. No, it seemed to him Gver Keleprai was the intended, the desecrator used to seal the matter, and perhaps to draw attention to his involvement and lead whatever investigation was sure to follow astray.

Directly from his meeting with the dancer he went to the Currlene House's storehouse in Lastl. He asked to speak with the Factor and was forced to stand waiting for over an hour watching the business of the day pass him by. The attendant who had first spoke to him studiously avoided his gaze as he led various people into the offices at the back. Hieran shifted from side to side, his legs and back aching, his fury growing. Finally, in a lull between visitors, the attendant appeared to take notice of him again and disappeared into the back.

He approached Hieran when he returned, nervously touching his hands together in greeting. "Are you waiting to see the Factor?" he asked.

"Yes. Nothing has changed since I walked through that door," Hieran said in exasperation. "Tell him I come with the seal of the Gver and I do not appreciate being made to wait to no reason."

"I'm afraid he is not here."

The Disciple stared in disbelief. "You told me earlier that he would see me."

"I was mistaken. I thought he was to come in this afternoon, but he is not."

"And you only thought to tell me now."

"I only just heard." The attendant glanced over his shoulder nervously.

"He is at his estate, then. I will go there."

"I'm afraid that also is not possible," the attendant said apologetically. "His eldest son is not well. He has the fevers. They will not be receiving anyone."

He paused, hoping that Hieran would draw the obvious conclusions. He decided not to. "I would like to see the junior Factor then, or whoever is in charge in the Factor's absence."

There was a further nervous glance behind. "That is not possible today. He is overwhelmed with work because the Factor is not here."

"Another time, then."

"Oh yes," the attendant agreed vigorously, relief flooding his features. "Yes, that is easily done."

They went over to his desk and he consulted his book and they settled on a time four days later. He could have gone and gotten some Magistery and returned to search the place or the Factor's estate, but he decided against it. Better perhaps to let them think this was a minor matter, an issue of unpaid customs or smuggling, than something of significance. Instead, the next day he sent one of Tehh's agents to watch the Factor's house while he went to settle in the tavern down the street and watch the storefront.

"Have faith in the infinite balance," he called to some passersby. "Join us and achieve a greater union of spirit and body. The Goddess smiles on her children."

They walked on, paying him no mind. So far all he had managed was a couple of lunes tossed at his feet. The real danger was if someone showed interest and stopped to question him. It would at least bring some excitement to what was proving to be a hot and dull day. Tehh felt that menial tasks were a benefit to his Disciples. How in the Gods' name would he know, Hieran asked himself.

He was in the midst of pondering this absurdity when he noticed the second Factor was leaving the storefront with a nobleman. He had noticed the man yesterday coming and going several times, the only person to do so, and finally had asked the tavern keeper if he knew who the fellow was. He couldn't see who the noble was, though, and he decided that this was worth abandoning his post for and set off behind them.

He didn't have to go far. They went just around the corner and hailed a palanquin. As they were seating themselves Hieran was able to see that the noble was Nes Ussul a Vellar, a cousin of Niriese ul Keleprai. He collected an image of the two and sent it to Tehh, falling in behind the palanquin as the porters lifted it to their shoulders and set off. They went north, taking a winding path and staying to the nameless avenues. He stayed well back on the opposite side of whatever street they happened to be on, trying to remain in amongst the crowds.

The Currlene storehouse was in Desnan, a section of the city filled with merchant and bank houses, and the palanquin passed by the lesser of these and beyond to Concubine Row. The palanquin moved quickly by the brothels and apartments where kept women spent their days, and Hieran was soon out of breath and cursing the porters. He threw Tehh into his string of invective as well, for making him do such demeaning work, for his noble birth, and for his denigration of his Disciple's poor birth. For that and innumerable other reasons.

He wondered what the two were after here. There were no innocent reasons to be in Concubine Row. If one wanted something in Lastl this was where you went, but that did not mean Ussul a Vellar was involved with the Apysel in a conspiracy against the Gver. He and the second Factor were of an age and conceivably their paths might have crossed previously. It was within the realm of possibility that this was merely to be an afternoon of pleasure.

Coincidence, though—coincidences and coincidences. The whole mess was going wider and deeper, and who knew when he would be able to get out of it. He cursed that too as the palanquin turned another corner onto a less-crowded street, the porters picking up speed in the open space. They turned quickly again and he broke into a jog to make sure he could see where they went. He was surprised to find himself in an alley that was quite narrow and filled with an overwhelming stench of indeterminate origins. The palanquin, he saw, was stopped at the alley's end.

His stomach fell away at the sight and he whirled around to see the entrance to the alley blocked and a man with a long Tuin dagger in his hand walking towards him. Hieran fumbled quickly in his Curedar robes for his own weapon. Before they engaged he sent an image of the alley, the palanquin, and his attacker to Tehh. Small good it would do him.

The man struck at him, moving with terrifying speed. Hieran did not even see the flash of the blade before it struck. He was saved by instinct alone, twisting away from the dagger, so violently that he threw himself against one of the buildings. The dagger caught him in the flesh where his shoulder met his chest, and he yelped in pain and was left gasping for air as his opponent drove his free hand into his stomach. He fell to his knees and then decided to go to ground entirely, hunching himself over into a ball before his attacker had a chance to pull out the dagger. The man stomped on his back in response.

"Cur."

Hieran had managed to lose his own dagger in his collapse, and he could only hope that it was somewhere underneath him. Or that the man did not have another weapon on him. Another blow from a boot rained down on him, this one up near his neck, driving his head into the ground. He grunted and came up tasting filth and blood. What he was waiting for came next as the man took a step around him to lay a boot into his head. He reached out with one hand, trying not to think of the foot that was descending upon his now exposed skull as he did so. His hand found his attacker's leg and he summoned whatever astral he could tear loose from the elements at hand, and then sent the seed of alkemy through to his attacker as though he were an Adept. The leg went rigid in his hand and he heard the man exhale in surprise before he went limp and collapsed to the ground.

Hieran scrambled to his feet to run, but the last blow had so stunned him that he nearly fell onto his attacker. He heard a yell from the palanquin at the other end of the alley and forced himself to go forward, though he wasn't even sure whether he was on his feet or crawling. He came weaving out of the alley and headed blindly down the street. Waves of color came at him, which he tried to blink away. It cleared a bit and he kept his momentum going, though the whole world was still very unsteady. He stumbled into the nearest alley he could find, hoping that it was on the opposite side of the street and that it did not have a dead end. His pursuers would have seen him, he was sure, so he kept going, moving in an awkward lope, his one hand heavy on the side of the building.

It came to a door, which opened, and he went in. He cursed his stupidity almost immediately. He had not gone down an alley but another street, for he was very plainly standing in an entryway to some sort of residence. He vaguely made out a set of stairs at the end of a hall. Standing before him were two very shocked women dressed in gaudy silks. The knife, he realized, was still sticking out of his chest.

Hieran smiled apologetically at them and glanced back at the door. Perhaps no one had seen him enter. *They will be able to follow the blood.* He turned back to see one of the women, the older of the two, walking out of the room, and he returned to his senses.

"Wait," he said and she stopped, waiting. "I am from the Palace. Whatever they offer I can exceed."

She stared at the protruding dagger. "And if you die?"

"They will honor it. The most powerful Adept Tehh will honor the price." He prayed to the Gods it was true.

He could see in her eyes when she made her decision. She nodded at the girl and then said, "Make sure to send Fesh and Kueren up front immediately."

The girl gestured for Hieran to follow, and he did, nearly stumbling on her heels in his haste. The two swords were idling at the bottom of the stairway, playing cards, and she sent them up front. One of them sighed audibly, noticing Hieran's additional appendage. They continued up the stairs and the girl led him into one of the rooms, though by this time Hieran had stopped paying attention to his surroundings, the swimming darkness falling in his eyes even as he walked. By the time he lay on the bed it had descended completely.

# 34

Lastl was the city of the spring fair. There were seven different ones before the Feast of Balance, each a time of song, tournament, and trade. The city was electric for those weeks, the days endless, all barriers between day and night cast asunder. Other barriers as well. In Keleprai's mind it was the final night of Suidene, the last and largest of the fairs, but memory sometimes conflated these things in favorable ways.

Of this he was sure: he had disguised himself as a woman, tying up his hair—long at the time as was the style—and blanketing his face heavily in paint so that he and Dalenna could spend the evening together in the midst of the revel without fear of one of the families noticing them. Most of the evening was lost to the shambles of the mind, the falling apart that happened at the edges of every recollection until they were only a series of disconnected instances.

There was one moment, though, that had stayed whole through all these long years. Twenty. It did not seem possible in so many ways. He had taken her into some alley just beyond the Auselem, the market and plaza where most of the celebrating occurred was, and there had fumbled in the darkness with his dress, trying to find his way through it. She had fallen to the ground, laughing uncontrollably and then, just as he began to get truly furious, her laughter had subsided and she had risen to her feet, and with her lips never leaving his, she had helped him.

This Keleprai thought about through the worst of the night,

watching the moon rise and fall over Lastl, the mythres in his bowl dwindling. Sleep finally found him as he sat in a chair, the cool of the darkness swimming over him, and there he stayed until the sun showed in the sky and the heat began to build chasing him inside.

A quiet desperation clung to Niriese ul Keleprai a Vellar, as if she knew already that her flaccid clawing at life as it ground away at her would all be for naught. Her breathing as she sat, propped up by mounds of pillows, in her bed was forced and shallow. Keleprai stood by her bedside in an awkward pose, unsure where to place himself as she stared at him, her eyes dull.

When it became clear she was not going to speak, he said, "What was Ussul doing with the second Factor of Currlene?"

Her expression did not change. "I am not my cousin's keeper."

"What was an Avellar doing with one of them? At the company warehouse, no less. Either he doesn't have an ounce of sense in him or he is in league with the Apysel."

"Listen to yourself," she said. "In league. He is young, who knows what he is thinking or doing."

He sighed, casting a glance around at the chairs behind him. "Do not pretend with me. You know there was an attempt on my life. All the evidence that we have gathered to this point suggests the Currlene were an involved party. And then, two days ago, someone sees Ussul with the second Factor and he is attacked while following them."

"Perhaps he shouldn't have been following palanquins without cause."

"Perhaps not. But that still does not explain what Ussul was doing. It is too much of a coincidence."

"I wished you showed as much concern for your own son," she said to him.

He threw up his hands in frustration, turning away from her. He said, striving to maintain a measured tone, "That is unfair. My own son is not conspiring against me, for one. And whatever else I am, I care for my heir."

A small smile passed by her lips and disappeared almost as quickly as it came. "Why would you assume that I would have such hate for you that I would be willing to throw away my son's future and my family's just to kill you?"

"I am left to assume it when your nephew is seen with my

enemies and the man who sees them is nearly killed for doing so."

"Whatever else I am, I have no need to stoop to murder. Our families have long been tied together and will be long after we are both in Ulternon's Hall, and you know as well as I there is nothing to be gained or done about it. You are nothing, what you have done in this realm and what you will do in the time left to you will amount to nothing, and you will be but a passing spirit in the hall. I have Rosteron to ensure me of my future. He will never be your son."

As they made their way down one of the passways, now freighted with danger, Keleprai asked the Master of Offices if there was anyone he trusted in his wife's company. When Nasyren mentioned someone, Keleprai told him, "Get what you can from them. See if you can find some others in her household who we might trust. I want to know who she sees and as much as what she has her servants doing as possible."

"It will be difficult, Most Gracious. Especially seeing what the servants do. They will find out we are following them," Nasyren said between heavy breaths. He was a short, heavyset man, growing thicker with age, and had never really grown used to keeping up with the longer strides of the Gver. It did not help that Keleprai now moved through the passways as quickly as possible, paying no mind as to whether he was able to keep up or not.

"I'm certain she will, she is nobody's fool. But it can't be helped." Then, his thoughts leading him in another direction, he asked, "Have you heard how the Disciple is doing?"

"Recovering is what the Adept told me yesterday. He should be fine, Most Immortal."

"They all recover quickly."

"They do indeed, my grace," Nasyren said, and then added, "They are strange creatures."

"They inhabit their own realm," the Gver agreed.

"In fact, Most Gracious," the Master of Offices said, "it was the strangest thing when I went to get Tehh after the attack. He already knew that the High Adept was with you."

Keleprai stopped and faced the Master of Offices. "What do you mean?"

"Just what I said, Most Immortal. When I went to see him, he was in his rooms. Someone was there, perhaps the Disciple, I don't remember. I asked to speak with him alone and told him that you had been attacked. And he asked if you had been wounded, and when I told him no, he asked whether his supremacy Cepedutherupt was unscathed as well."

"And you are absolutely certain you had not mentioned the High Adept to him before he asked?"

"Absolutely, Gver. Absolutely." The Master of Offices had gone pale, the arm which had held up the lantern slumped down to his side, the light and shadow vibrating madly about the passage.

"I did not think of it at the time, Most Gracious. I was more worried about everything else, you understand. And I did not even think of it again until now. But he knew, he knew the High Adept was there. And I guess I just assumed that you had told him, or that they knew these sort of things about each other."

"Indeed," Keleprai said, glancing about at the encroaching darkness as though there were hidden threats there even now. He turned back to Nasyren and their eyes met for a moment.

"Lift the lantern a bit," the Gver said.

"Yes, Most Immortal," the Master of Offices replied, and they made their way down the passage.

# 35

Gethuul had remained on board the vessel following his losses at the card table, though now he had nowhere to go, unless it was home to Estuen, and no coin even to eat. The night before he had slept on the servants' vessel, the second inviting him aboard out of pity, though it remained to be seen how far that pity would be extended. Vyissan had kept his distance from the man, unsure how he would react now that the ruins of his life lay all around him, but Gethuul had been so disconsolate he hardly noticed or acknowledged those who offered him kindness.

The Ad Feina had left in a flourish that morning, just as he had arrived, talking loudly as he went of how he would dispatch one of his men to handle this business with assenta flowers. Vyissan stood with another merchant, watching as the Ad Feina yelled at his slaves for a palanquin. "Strange that his business should take him here," he said to the other, giving voice to a thought that had come to him as he eyed the unremarkable river village that the Ad Feina had chosen to disembark at.

"Strange indeed," the merchant said with a laugh. "The robes may fit, but that doesn't mean he should be wearing them."

At midday they passed a village that had been razed the night before, its remains still smoking. A crowd gathered on the starboard side of the boat to gaze and murmur at the ruins. There were corpses near the river bank that had not been consumed by the fire, though the birds and other creatures had been at them, and it was clear at a glance that they had been taken to the sword.

The entrails of one poor soul, split wide by an attacker, had been dragged all along the shoreline. All the boats on the dock had also been burned or capsized and their shattered hulls were just visible beneath the surface of the river. The stench of charred flesh was still in the air.

"Why would they do this?" one man said to no one in particular, and was greeted with silence. Someone wanted to go to the captain to have some of their guards search the shore for anyone who had escaped the attackers.

"Are you mad?" another replied. "What if they're still out there?"

"We should do something for those people there. Ancestors guide us, we should do something. That captain has done nothing this whole trip but stay below deck doing ancestors know what."

In the end nothing was done; they all stayed watching as the boat continued upriver, the ruined village disappearing from view. Vyissan drifted from the group to the aft of the ship, where he would most often sit to sketch. He half listened as others discussed what they had seen. There was talk of Shadow Men conspiracies, the advisers of the Ad Eselte, or various heads of important families replaced by the Shadows and acting out their aims.

He almost smiled. And to the think, here he was in their midst, the very creature they dreaded. He would not begrudge them their fear, for look what he was bringing them, and to what end. How strange and petty this quarrel over alkemyas and engines must seem to a people who rejected it all.

The Gods, it was said, had created a world imbalanced, the substance of their creations imperfectly scaled between their two aspects, the elemental and the astral. It was given to the most skilled of their favored creatures, the Adepts, the means, the art, to bring the aspects of this realm to balance. The reward for them was both spiritual and profane. The spiritual was obvious, all creation desired balance in all aspects, and the profane was the germ of alkemy formed from the decayed astral, from death to a new being. A fine and exacting art, something only achieved by those with the innate talent for it and the skill gained through years of training by the Council.

That had been the wisdom on the matter until Kercubegahedd and his quicksilver engines. Now, the Council Adepts said, a thing's astral substance could be drawn without heed to balance, to any concern for the realms of existence, without any need to fear the maintenance of the balance within. Quicksilver had been known and feared for centuries as an element so out of balance it could inhabit all constitutions simultaneously and decay the astral substance of anything it came near. Kercubegahedd and his minions had compounded this innate evil by setting them in engines, which forced the element to simultaneity allowing its inherent anarchy to blossom beyond measure.

And in doing so, he set men free. No more did one man have to submit to another as a Disciple. The Council spoke of balance, but they held the scale, Kercubegahedd had said.

But what did these things matter if the whole act of it was a negation of what it meant to be a soul alive in this realm? Vyissan would not blame anyone for thinking that, not after the things he had witnessed. The things he had done in the few short years he had practiced this art, Nesyur being but the latest casualty. And to what end would it all serve? It all seemed so small, measured against the size of the realms he had passed through, the span of their days but a breath compared to all those that had come and all those that would follow.

At what cost had he done all these things? His soul was impure and that would be accounted for when he came to doors of Ulternon's hall. And what had his sacrifice, and those to come, achieved? He thought again of the ruins in the desert, the forgotten of existence.

The city came into view at dusk, a creature sprawled along the river with a patchwork coat of glimmering light and darkness. It was an awesome thing to witness, the walls stretching on beyond view to the west, the docks more extensive than any of the ocean ports in Craitol, and the city beyond the wall on the other side of the river spilling out of the valley to the east like the belly of a gorged beast. The walls were taller than any he had seen, the tallest in all the Realms if the songs were to be believed. And there were walls within the walls, he had heard. The Shadow Men's raid was all the more amazing, seeing this firsthand. What surprised him most was that he could see the bejeweled domes of the Imperial Palace from wherever they lay within the city over the great walls flaring in the dying sun. An empire within the Empire, they said, and he could see why.

Now he would have to traverse it. He had thought that once he got himself to Darrhyn it would be easier, the difficult part of the journey completed, but now that he was here a heavy foreboding settled on him. It seemed he had only begun his task, not reached its end. As the slaves pulled them into the docks and they prepared to disembark, he could still glimpse the domes glittering in the final moments of daylight.

# GLOSSARY OF TERMS

Abapolly: mythical demon from Kragi

Ad Eselte: title of emperor in Renuih

Adept: practioner of alkemya

Aesen: canal in Darrhyn

Alkemy: the latent power within all elements that can be released by transmutation

Alkemya: the practice and study

Anchonites: monastic priest in Renuih

Ardeh: animal, raised for its wool, milk and meat

Asieren: Ad Ezern paradise in Renuih

Aslyn: leaf that is chewed

Astral: aspect of elements that contains alkemy

Asyl: psychotropic nectar

Ceinobyte: Renian priest

Celes: Ad Reteln paradise in Renuih

Cohort: Craitolian amy unit

Corenedor: Renian officer in the army or Watch

Craitol: Realm of, as well as capital of the Realm; westernmost realm in all the lands

Cureders: Craitolian priest

Dala: beans, drink brewed from

Darrhyn: imperial city of Renuih

Devew:city and river in Kragi

Disciple: practitioner of alkemya, Adept's subordinate

Dravasyl: drinkery in Darrhyn

Elen: city in Renuih

Enir: a distinct religious sect of the Renian people

Enir Republics: once part of Renuih; now independent city states along the coast between Renuih and Craitol, south of the desert; inhabited by those of the Enir sect

Eresnan: River between Darrhyn and Sylaron in Renuih

Esyln: jewel of the Renian Empire in the desert; now a ruins inhabited by the Shadow Men

Fegh: city in Kragi Province

Gver: Craitolian lord, governor of a particular territory

Haigah: mountain city on the border between Kragi and Craitol; a mountain pass

The Hashil: central boulevard in Lastl

Hasierren: Lasisen sanctuary in Craitol

Hessen: Enir Republic

Hesite: district in Takyl

Hezier: ruler in the Enir Republics

Hueithel: neighborhood in Darrhyn

Isinan: a street in Darrhyn

Kastril: Renian fruit

Kenir: coin of Renuih

Kragi: province in the north of Craitol; once an independent realm

Kulez: northern city in Renuih

Kylep: city in Craitol; seat of a Gver Byuvir

Lasisen: a sect of worshipers of Senteur in Craitol

Lastl: city in Craitol; seat of a Gver Keleprai

Lethle: city in Kragi Province

Luessan: one of the three eastern kingdoms that broke away from the Renuih Empire

Luisel: town in Renuih

Magister: officer of law in Craitol

Magisterium: building of the Magistery

Magistery: officers, or the office itself

Melinon: Craitolian goddess of the earth

Mgetir: island south of Craitol

Morning, Midday, Evening: factions in Craitol

Mythres: powder made from flowers native to Kragi

Nrai: port city in Craitol; one of the contestants in the Sea Challenge; seat of Gver Assuard

Nohritai: nobility in Renuih

Nuerrallah: one of the great sages of Reniuh

Qraul: ruler of Craitol

Quadra: unit of the armed forces in Renuih

Quicksilver: an element capable of inhabiting all constitutions simultaneously and decaying the astral of any substance

Pyrsedies: forts guarding the desert frontier in Craitol

Psyel: city in Craitol; seat of Gver Pervelte

Rakai: port city in Craitol; involved in Sea Challenge

Renuih: Empire in the east, former rulers of the desert

Sanader: religious authority in Craitol; usually has authority over a particular city or region

Senteur: Craitolian god of the heavens

Shadow Men: the people of the desert; also referred to as Shadows or by other pejoratives (demons, beasts, etc.)

Suliher: honorific for those in the Renian Watch or Army

Sylaron: major port city in Renuih

Takyl: city in Craitol; seat of Gver Duirhe

Tolote: coyote-like animal of the desert

Tson: city in Craitol; seat of Gver Hythel

Tuissar: Enir Republic

Uenam: district in Darrhyn

Ulternon: Craitolian god of the dead

Usgelt: city in Kragi Province

Vazeir: imperial administrator in Renuih

Watch: protectors of the imperial city Darrhyn

Xln: port city in Craitol, involved in Sea Challenge

Yuehilth: prison in Darrhyn

Yseltez: city in Craitol; seat of Gver Issilar

# ABOUT THE AUTHOR

Clint Westgard is the author of The Shadow Men Trilogy and the science fiction epic The Sojourner Cycle, the first volume of which, The Forgotten, was published in 2015. In addition, he has published a work of historical fantasy set in colonial Peru, *The Maleficio Chronicles*, and a retelling of the Minotaur legend, *The Trials of the Minotaur*. Clint Westgard lives in Calgary, Alberta.

# ALSO BY CLINT WESTGARD

*Council of Shadows*

*Volume Two of The Shadow Men*


Discontent continues to fester within the realms of Craitol and Renuih, fed by intrigues carried out in the shadows. As rivals and apostates struggle for supremacy, a long incubated plan begins to unfold.


Vyissan, a mysterious alkemycal practitioner arrives in Renuih, the latest strike in a long war over who shall control the secrets of alkemya and Craitol itself. He carries with him a secret that, once revealed, will reverberate across all realms. Before he can reveal it though, the conspirators against the emperor will strike their own blow.


But now, a new and more powerful menace looms on the horizon. The Shadow Men have gained the secrets of the Council Adept's alkemya and no one can be certain what they will do with it...

# ALSO BY CLINT WESTGARD

*Dance of Shadows*
*Volume Three of The Shadow Men*


War with the Shadow Men looms in both realms as the
consequences of the Gvers' Council in Craitol begin to make
themselves known. A war that could end in glorious triumph or
bitter disaster.


Doubt shadows everyone's steps, for they know there are no
certainties in the desert. Especially now the Shadow Men have
made the art of alkemya their own.


No one has more questions than Vyissan, for he is working in
service to a cause he is no longer sure he believes in. And now he
must undertake a journey with those who both loathe and fear him.
Before the first sword is drawn, his life will be under threat.


But his will not be the only one, for somewhere in the desert the
Shadow Men lie in wait...

# ALSO BY CLINT WESTGARD

*The Forgotten*

*Volume One of The Sojourners Cycle*


Who is David Aeida? And what does he know that has so many
people pursuing him?


David doesn't know. He can't remember anything about who he is.
But he finds himself ensnared in a vicious conflict between a
religious cult and a guild that patrols the crossings between
multiple universes. They will both stop at nothing to gain whatever
knowledge he possesses. Most dangerous of all, is the implacable
hunter, known only as the Seeker, who has his own reasons for
wanting to find David.


His only hope is to recover his memories before they do. His only
ally is a woman named Meredith, and she definitely knows more
than she is telling…


Spanning both universes and the human mind, *The Forgotten* is an
unforgettable science fiction thriller that questions the very nature
of identity. It is the first volume of the *Sojourners Cycle*, an epic that
will encompass the fates of universes and humanity itself.

# ALSO BY CLINT WESTGARD

*The Maleficio Chronicles*

Luisa is always more than she appears. Rumor and mystery surround her. And strange events seem to follow wherever she goes.

Born in Lima, City of Kings, to a noble family, her father so fears her true nature that he banishes her to a convent. There she falls under the suspicion of the Inquisition and decides to flee.

Disguised as a man, she embarks upon a series of wild adventures, dueling, carousing, and gambling her way across colonial Peru. But everything changes when someone recognizes her for what she truly is, and soon she finds herself fighting for her very survival.

In a world where she will always stand apart, Luisa undergoes a strange journey, marked by betrayal and murder, terrible powers and mysterious strangers. *The Maleficio Chronicles* is her incredible confession and a story like no other.

# ALSO BY CLINT WESTGARD

*The Trials of the Minotaur*

In the fifth year of the rule of Auten the One Eyed a minotaur is born to one of Colosi's most important families.

Taken from his mother as a newborn, exiled and cast from his family, the minotaur vows to return to the imperial city and take his rightful place as a patrician in the empire. But the patriarch of the family, his grandfather, will stop at nothing to see this blemish to his honor destroyed.

And so begins an epic journey, through lands beyond imagining, marked by despair and exile, triumph and betrayal. At its heart lies a quest to be free.